Cinnamon Girl

Looking
For A Hero

Cathy Hopkins is the author of the incredibly successful *Mates, Dates* and *Truth, Dare* books, as well as the highly acclaimed *Cinnamon Girl* series. She lives in North London with her husband and cats.

Cathy spends most of her time locked in a shed at the bottom of the garden pretending to write books, but she is actually in there listening to music, hippie dancing and talking to her friends on email.

Apart from that, Cathy has joined the gym and spends more time than is good for her making up excuses as to why she hasn't got time to go.

Find out more about Cathy and her books at
www.cathyhopkins.com

Cathy Hopkins

Cinnamon Girl

Looking
For A Hero

PICCADILLY PRESS * LONDON

*I'd like to dedicate this book to Steve Lovering,
my own hero, who took many years to find.
Thanks as always to Brenda Gardner, Anne Clark,
Melissa Patey and all the fab team at Piccadilly
who make doing these books such a pleasure.*

First published in Great Britain in 2008
by Piccadilly Press Ltd,
5 Castle Road, London NW1 8PR
www.piccadillypress.co.uk

A catalogue record for this book is available from the British Library

ISBN: 978 1 85340 975 2

3 5 7 9 10 8 6 4

Printed in the UK by CPI Bookmarque, Croydon, CR0 4TD
Text design by Carolyn Griffiths, Cambridge
Cover design by Simon Davis
Cover illustration by Sue Hellard'

Chapter 1

Love Is in the Air

'How do you know when you're in love?' asked Leela as she kicked her feet through the carpet of autumn leaves on the way to Starbucks for an after-school hot chocolate.

'You have butterflies in your tummy. You feel light-headed and your legs go to jelly when you see him,' said Brook, offering round a packet of Liquorice Allsorts, then taking one herself.

Zahrah pulled her collar up against the chill wind. 'Sounds like some kind of disease,' she said. 'One that you should avoid at all costs or at least take some supplements to stop you catching.'

'*Lo-ove is the bug that I'm dreaming of,*' sang Brook and she popped a pink Allsort into her mouth then linked her arm through mine. I linked my other arm with Zahrah and she linked with Leela. I glanced along the line at my new friends. I still couldn't believe my luck – I'd only started at our school in September and had spent the first few weeks feeling like a Molly-no-Mates, but then, over the half-term, I'd got in with this great bunch of girls who were a real laugh. It was now nearly the end of October and I felt like I'd known them all my life.

As we walked along, I could see a few boys from the Sixth Form checking us out – my new friends are an attractive bunch, all brunettes apart from me. My hair is more red chestnut than dark.

'We're an exotic lot,' Brook had said one evening when we were talking about our families and the various places we'd lived before ending up in Notting Hill in London. I won the 'most travelled prize' hands down – my family has lived in five different countries since I was born (India, the Caribbean, Morocco, Italy and Ireland). Brook came second. Both her parents are American and she lived in New York until she moved to London with her mum when she was eleven. She's still got a slight American accent. She recently chopped her hair to a jaw length bob and it really shows off her beautiful heart-shaped face and her grey-green eyes that always seem so thoughtful. Leela is from an Indian background but was born here in the UK in Leicester. Her family moved to London when she was six. She's the smallest of the four of us with delicate features and long hair that shines like silk when she wears it loose but most of the time she wears it back in a clip. Zahrah is from a mixed background – Ethiopian on her mum's side and English on her dad's. She grew up in the East End of London before moving to Queen's Park where her family live now. She's the same height as I am (five foot nine), and has high cheek bones and huge dark brown eyes with eyelashes that are so long and curly they almost look false. Her aunt does her hair for her, in plaited cornrows close to her head. One day, when I know Zahrah better, I'm going to ask her if her aunt will do mine in little plaits. At the moment, my hair's shoulder-length in layers and I think it's boring. I'd like to do something mad with it, like dye it white-blonde for a change. I was going to do it one weekend but Mum talked me out of it saying that the red tones in my hair suit my eyes which are amber. I'd love to be a blonde with blue eyes, at least for a couple of weeks.

'What do you think, India Jane?' asked Leela as we reached Starbucks and she pushed open the door. A blast of warm air that smelled of roasted coffee hit us as we trooped in after her. We quickly bagged the two leather sofas by the window where you get the best view of the boys coming out of the private school down the road. I immediately thought about Joe Donahue. I'd first seen him sitting here when I'd arrived in London back in the summer and thought that if he was a typical example of the local boys then I'd landed in heaven. A lot had happened since then and Joe and I had been on our first date last weekend. Well, sort of date. Actually it was a trip to an art gallery to see an exhibition by a local artist who my Aunt Sarah rates and, OK, so Aunt Sarah and Joe's mum were there too (they work together), but he took my hand and stroked my fingers when they went off to buy something from the gallery shop and we were alone for a few minutes. It sent shivers up and down my spine and I thought that, in a funny way, you can kiss with your hands. I felt all the butterflies and jelly-leg symptoms that Brook had just mentioned. So, oh yes, it was definitely love as far as I was concerned when it came to Joe.

'You feel on a high,' I said as I put my rucksack in the corner of the sofa. 'You want to be your best self and you can't stop thinking about him and even the slightest touch, like brushing hands or arms, can make you feel all warm and fluttery inside.'

'Joe?' asked Zahrah.

I nodded.

She took a sharp breath in.

'Oh I know all about his bad-boy reputation,' I said. 'Don't worry. And I really think he's over that.'

Zahrah sucked in the air through her teeth making a hissing sound and pinched her mouth tight with disapproval. I laughed. Although I'd only been hanging around with Zahrah, Brook and Leela for the couple of weeks since half-term, I had quickly learned that sometimes Zahrah didn't speak, rather she let her face say what she was thinking. She even used her breath to communicate: she let out long sighs if she was unhappy, short sighs if bored and irritated and the sharp intake of breath meant watch out, beware or that she really *really* didn't approve.

'Yeah, yeah, I know,' I said, smiling at her, 'but I really do think it's different with us. I can feel it. Now who wants what?'

'Hot chocolate,' said Leela.

'Herbal for me,' said Brook. 'Peppermint.'

'Cappuccino for me,' said Zahrah. 'I'll come with you.'

We made our way to the counter and joined a queue made up of other pupils from our school in the same black and white uniform. Choosing to speak in Zahrah's language, I let out a sigh of happiness.

'Someone's in a good mood,' she commented.

I was. Life was good. I had three fab new girl friends. Joe Donahue was maybe my boyfriend and love was in the air.

'I know,' I said and I gave her arm a squeeze. 'I love the autumn, don't you? The crisp chill air and the smell of bonfires and damp leaves when the light fades. Wrapping up in scarves and gloves. Going home and getting cosy by the fire.'

Zahrah shrugged and gave me an 'Are you bonkers?' look. 'I need the sun,' she said. 'I'm sure I get that SAD condition in the winter.' She slumped her shoulders and made her face look so miserable that I almost laughed. I didn't because I was still getting to know her and didn't want to offend her in case she was being serious. 'Seasonal Affective Disorder. It's because my family are from the sunshine land.'

'Oh yeah. Africa. Have you ever been there?'

'No. Not yet. I'd like to. Mum goes back when she can but it would be too expensive for us all to go. Like six air fares if Dad came too. Can you imagine? But I can feel Africa is in my blood – that's probably why I don't like the cold weather.'

I had an urge to say something silly about it being painful

having a whole continent in one's blood but I bit it back. I felt slightly in awe of Zahrah. She came across as very cool and sure of herself and what she thought of the world, and I needed to get to know her better before I showed my daft side. We reached the part of the counter that displayed the cakes and pastries and got distracted for a moment by the fudge pecan cookies. On top of the glass counter, I noticed a chocolate bar with a red wrapper. It said it was cinnamon chocolate. *I'll get that for Joe,* I thought as I reached out for it. Zahrah raised an eyebrow as if questioning my purchase.

'Not for me,' I said. 'For Joe.'

She raised her other eyebrow but I wasn't sure exactly what that meant. *I must ask my cousin Kate for tips so that I can communicate more fluently Zahrah-style – she also does the eyebrow speak,* I thought as the queue moved along.

'It will remind him of me because it's cinnamon flavoured. My mate Erin always said that it's good to give boys things that remind them of you.'

Zahrah gave me a quizzical look.

'Dad calls me Cinnamon Girl —'

Zahrah nodded and pulled gently on my hair with her right hand and looked into my eyes. 'Hmm. Spice colours,' she said. 'Fits.'

I nodded back. 'And my mum makes me a perfume for my birthday which has cinnamon in it and I had it on once when I was sitting next to Joe and he said he liked it.'

'Hmm. That's good.'

'Yeah. Mum says that smell is a very potent sense and that it is important to find your signature scent and stick to it so that every time anyone smells it, they're reminded of you. My mum's worn the same perfume all her life, since she was a teenager and, whenever I smell it, it makes me think of her.'

I could just imagine the scene. It would be so romantic. I'd give Joe the chocolate. He would smile, smell the aroma of cinnamon and cocoa, nuzzle into my neck and then promise to keep the chocolate bar for ever. It would be the first of many special mementos I'd give him in the course of our relationship.

'So why not give him some of the perfume?'

'Too girlie – although maybe I could send him a card that is scented with it for his birthday, but that's not until February. He's an Aquarian.' I looked down at the chocolate bar. 'But I can't go wrong with this, can I? The cinnamon will remind him of me plus it tastes good.'

'Wow. You've really got it bad, haven't you?'

I raised an eyebrow and smiled. That was my silent way of saying, *Oh yeah*. She got it.

'Good luck,' she said as the person behind the counter looked our way, ready to take our order.

As soon as I got home later, I went up to my room to start work on the scenery designs – I had an hour spare before I'd arranged to talk to Erin on MSN. She's my mate from my old school in Ireland and is my best friend in the world. I missed her like mad when I first moved to London and it was actually

7

thanks to her that I got in with Leela, Brook and Zahrah. Erin visited at half-term and soon made friends with them and got an invite for us to a Bollywood party at Leela's house. In fact, her whole visit was good because I'd been put in charge of scenery for *The Boy Friend*, the school end-of-term show and I had been agonising over what theme we should take. At first, I'd come up with ideas that had already been used for previous school shows and I could see that the scenery team were having serious doubts about me being in charge. And then, at Leela's party, I suddenly realised that Bollywood should be the theme and everyone loved the idea. All in all, I had a lot to be thankful to Erin for; she was a true friend.

I settled down at my desk and started work on preliminary designs for the scenery. Aunt Sarah had found me a fab book full of examples of the colours and designs used in Indian films and I spent an hour copying and drawing up some basic designs to take to the next scenery meeting. Bright pink, lime green and orange seemed to be the main colours needed for a Bollywood look, with a healthy addition of silver and gold glitter thrown in.

When I'd finished, I saw that it was the prearranged time to talk to Erin on MSN so I moved on to my computer. She was already there and waiting for me.

Irishbrat4eva: So my deario. How goes it in the land of red, white and blue?

Cinnamongirl: Most excellent. How goes it with you?

Irishbrat4eva: Not sure. Saw my liege, yon Scott the brave on the way back from school and methinks he is acting somewhat poxy.

(Erin and I speak our own Shakespearian made-up language.)

Cinnamongirl: Poxy how?

Irishbrat4eva: He hath been acting a bit weirdiedoodie of late methinks. Maybe he ist worried about something but I suspect he may be making merry too much with his fellow lords who like yon ale and acting like yon pissheads.

Cinnamongirl: Those who suppeth too much can be loud and boring.

Irishbrat4eva: Thou speakest the truth indeedie doo. How is Lord Joe of the house of Donahue?

Cinnamongirl: Methinks he will be my liege before the week is over. Tis true love that beats upon mine breast oh yay yay and thrice times yahey and a wahey too. Hey, how do you think you know when it's the real thing, Erin?

Irishbrat4eva: You just know. It's a feeling that it's right and a little cherub appears over your head and fires an arrow at you capow and your heart doth go, lalalalala. Cabung, cabung.

Cinnamongirl: Yon Cupid hast most deffo fired yon arrows into minest heart all right. Do you love Scott?

Irishbrat4eva:	Fie that thou could thinkst so. I fanciest Scott but he is not boyfriend material, hey nonny no. He ist headmessing material, like if a wench would get serious over him, he would do her head in so I must stayeth cool. How are your new pals?
Cinnamongirl:	Great. I totally love them. Love hanging out with them.
Irishbrat4eva:	Fie on them, thou art my friend though I knowest that they are cool, but I miss you. Boo hooest.
Cinnamongirl:	A moment fair lady, lend me your ear for methinks me hears the door bell. Forsooth, indeed, it is. There art someone at the door.
Irishbrat4eva:	Go forth and see who stands there and anyway, my supper calleth and my stomach doth rumbleth. Later.
Cinnamongirl:	Laters.

I logged off and flew down the stairs as no one else was home. Mum, Dad and Dylan had gone to an early movie, my cousin Kate never answers the door even when she is in and Aunt Sarah was out working. I opened the door and my stomach did a double flip.

Standing at the door was a vision of boy handsomeness. Tall, broad-shouldered, wide-mouthed, smiley-eyed. Joe.

'Ah . . . oh . . . hi . . .' I panted and tried to regain my breath, smooth my hair and look cool all at the same time.

It clearly didn't work. 'Been running?' he asked.

'Was u . . . uh upstairs.'

'Can I come in?'

'Sure,' I said and stood aside for him. I was so chuffed that he'd come over to see me. I showed him into the living room at the front of the house. He followed me in and hovered by the fireplace. The atmosphere felt awkward then I remembered the chocolate bar I'd bought for him.

'Oh, I have something for you,' I said.

'Me? Thanks and —'

'Back in a sec,' I said and raced upstairs. *He was about to say something,* I thought as I grabbed the bar from my rucksack, then charged back down the stairs, into the living room and thrust it in his hand.

'For you,' I said. 'You were about to say something, sorry. Go ahead.'

Joe looked at the chocolate bar. 'Oh. Cinnamon chocolate. That's different. Thanks. Um. Yes.'

'What were you about to say?'

'Is it to eat or look at?'

'Eat. I, er . . . cinnamon . . .' Suddenly my speech about wanting to give him something to remind him of me sounded presumptuous.

Joe thumped his forehead with the palm of his hand. 'Oh right. Cinnamon. You're Cinnamon Girl, right? Yeah. That's sweet.'

'Yeah. Sweet. Chocolate usually is.'

Suddenly I wanted to die. I wanted the ground to open up

and swallow me. I shouldn't have bought him the chocolate. It was too much, too soon to buy him a gift. We weren't even dating properly. I needed to make light of it.

I took the chocolate back from him and ripped open the paper. 'Want a bit?'

Joe gave me a strange look. 'Isn't that like taking grapes to someone in hospital then sitting and eating them all?'

'No. How? You're not in hospital.'

'I know. Just . . .' Joe sighed.

'It's not a gift or anything. I just bought it on the way home and wanted to try it and I was about to and then you arrived and . . .' I knew I was rambling.

'Go on then, give us a bit.'

I snapped off two sections, handed one to him and put the other piece in my mouth. We stood there chewing, but it felt like I was eating glue. I wanted Joe to go. *Why is it so uncomfortable?* I asked myself. We'd been getting on so well lately.

'I . . .' I began.

Joe burst out laughing.

'What?' I asked.

He pointed at my mouth. *Oh God, I've smeared chocolate like a five-year-old,* I thought as I walked over to the mirror above the fireplace to see the damage.

'Tooth,' said Joe.

I hadn't smeared it. A blob of it had stuck over one of my teeth on the top row, giving me the appearance of missing a tooth. Toothless. Like an old witch.

Joe came and stood behind me. 'Hmm, that's an interesting look.' For a second, our eyes met in the mirror and I thought he was going to pull me back to lean against him and even nuzzle into my neck and I felt my insides melt, but then we heard someone at the front door, footsteps in the hall, and Aunt Sarah came in.

'Hello you two,' she said.

Joe stepped back, reached into his pocket, pulled out an envelope and handed it to her. 'Mum asked me to drop this into you,' he said.

'Thanks, Joe,' said Aunt Sarah.

Oh God. He hadn't even come to see me. My humiliation is now complete, I thought as I licked over my teeth with my tongue then stood there like an idiot.

Chapter 2

Looking for a Hero

A week later and Joe hadn't called nor had I bumped into him at school – although that wasn't unusual as he was in the Sixth Form and they had their own common room. He wasn't even at the scenery meeting on Saturday morning when I handed over my Bollywood designs. Harry, one of the guys on the team, said Joe'd called him and said that he couldn't make the meeting and, although everyone loved the designs, I felt peeved that Joe hadn't let me know that he wasn't going to be there.

After the meeting, I met Leela and Zahrah and we went around to Brook's house to find Brook's mum was busy on the Internet looking for a boyfriend on a dating website.

'I'm looking for a hero,' she'd said when we blew in from outside (it was wet and windy) and gathered around the laptop. 'You can help.'

'Have you put your photo on?' I asked.

She shook her head and opened a file on the computer showing some photos of herself. She was very attractive for an older lady in her forties, sophisticated with glossy dark hair like Brook's and a slim figure. I didn't think she'd find it hard to meet a man. We glanced over the photos and I pointed at one showing her leaning against a gate in the countryside wearing jeans and a white shirt with the sleeves rolled up.

'I like that one,' I said. 'You look relaxed in it.'

Brook frowned and pointed at the screen at one of her mum in a bikini on a beach. 'You mustn't put that up – God only knows what response you'd get.'

'I'm proud of my body, hon,' said Mrs Holmes. 'I work hard at it.'

'Well, I don't want you flaunting it on the Internet,' said Brook. I laughed. She sounded so prim.

Mrs Holmes clicked on to the part of the website that showed men's profiles and scrolled though them as we looked on.

'Ergh, not him,' said Brook as a heavy-set man appeared on the screen. 'Come on, Mom, think about this. I mean, one of these guys might be my new stepdad and that guy you're checking out looks like he'd chop you into pieces, eat your liver then bury your remains under the floorboards.'

'Yeah. Creepy,' said Leela with a shudder as Mrs Holmes moved to a man with a neat white beard, close-set eyes and thin mouth.

'Delete,' said Zahrah. A chubby Elvis look-a-like was grinning at us.

Next a pleasant-looking man with short silver hair popped up on the screen. 'Oh, he looks nice,' Leela and I chorused.

'He's a biologist,' said Mrs Holmes, reading his profile. 'Hmm, so he's got a brain.'

'You hope,' said Zahrah.

'I do,' said Mrs Holmes. She smiled at a photo of a man in a diving suit. 'This one sounds like a laugh. *Have my own teeth and hair, don't give up on me. I like to have fun and am looking for a lady I can do exactly that with.*'

'I think you should be very careful,' said Zahrah. 'You don't know who these men are.'

'Oh, don't worry,' said Mrs Holmes. 'I know the rules. Always meet in a public place. Don't give out personal details like your address or phone number.'

'Or where you work,' added Zahrah. 'Or even the year you were born – people can use personal details like that. Fraudsters steal identities from the Web.'

Mrs Holmes laughed. 'Shouldn't it be me telling you girls this? You lot are like a bunch of old women. Honestly!'

'I wouldn't look for a boy on the Net,' said Zahrah. 'Too many nutters out there.'

'Well you're young and meeting people all the time,' said Mrs Holmes. 'It's different when you get to my age. All my friends are in couples and they've already introduced me to all their single friends. And it can happen. My friend at work met someone online last year and they're very happy together.'

'Aren't there any men at your work?' asked Leela. (Mrs

16

Holmes runs a gallery in Mayfair that imports American art.)

'Only married or gay. There aren't any eligible ones in my world. No. I move with the times and the Internet it is,' said Mrs Holmes. 'It's fun and it makes me realise that I have choice. Don't worry Brook, I don't have to marry any of them. Or even snog them.'

'Yerghh, *Mom*. Too much information,' said Brook. The screen scrolled down to a man who looked like an old woman with bouffant white hair. 'Ohmigod, not him! Or is it a her?'

'I think it's brave that these people put themselves up to be judged like this,' said Leela. 'I think they must be the sort of people who have a positive attitude to life.'

'Well you would, little Miss Trust Everybody,' said Zahrah. 'You think everyone is wonderful.'

'I agree with Leela,' said Mrs Holmes. 'It's brave to do something like this. So go easy on them and me. Now who's going to make me a cup of herbal tea while I sort out the man of the moment?'

'I will,' I said, and got up to go to the kettle.

It was fun hanging at Brook's. She and her mum have a fabbie-dabbie place in Holland Park. It's even posher than my aunt's house and that's impressive. I still thank God Aunt Sarah invited my family to stay when Mum and Dad ran out of money – I don't think we could have afforded more than a studio flat out in the sticks. Mrs Holmes's flat even smells expensive as she always has Jo Malone candles burning and the scent of jasmine or lily of the valley permeates the rooms. Apparently Brook's father is mega rich, and when he and her mother divorced, Mrs Holmes got a ton of dosh in the settlement and that was when she and Brook left New York, came over here and bought this awesome flat. It's very Manhattan chic – huge light rooms, floor to ceiling windows and white walls displaying some of the art that Brook's mum deals with. Some of it looks to me like it was painted by a five-year-old having a tantrum, but Brook says that her mum has her finger on the pulse and buys up-and-coming artists' work as an investment. I hope one day she'll buy mine. Brook said that I should show her some of my drawings, but I'm not ready to. I couldn't bear it if she hated them.

Leaving Mrs Holmes to search the Net for Mr Right, Zahrah, Brook, Leela and I went up to Brook's bedroom. Unlike the rest of the house, which was modern and minimal, Brook's room looked like it belonged to a fairy princess. It even had a four-poster bed draped in white muslin with pearly sequins on it. Mucho chav, apart from the vast collection of books on the tall shelf unit to the right of the window. It suited Brook's romantic personality perfectly.

Leela threw herself on the bed, propped herself up on her elbow and said, 'I do hope your mum finds the perfect man.'

Brook shrugged. 'Perfect man? Who would he be?'

'A Buddha with balls and a Bentley,' I said. I'd heard my Aunt Sarah say that was the definition of her perfect man.

Zahrah cracked up. 'Hmm. Somehow I don't think she's going to find *him* on the Internet.'

'She might,' said Leela. 'At least she's looking. She hasn't given up.'

'She could Google him,' I said. 'Buddha with balls. See what comes up.'

'Knowing Mom, she already has,' said Brook gravely.

'I think *we* should make a list of what we want in a boy,' said Leela. 'Have you got any paper?'

'I have, but I'm not sure I've got *enough*. My list is going to be so long – I'm very picky,' said Brook. She went over to a chest of drawers, rummaged around and found some paper. She handed us all a sheet and a pen.

'Now,' said Leela. 'We each have to write a list.'

'Bossy boots,' said Zahrah and she settled herself next to Leela on the bed while Brook and I flopped on to the two white velvet beanbags on the floor by the window. 'I don't want a boy.'

'You will one day,' said Leela. 'So it's good to be ready. OK. Start with looks.'

'Nice-looking,' I said.

'Be specific,' said Leela. 'Nice-looking how?'

I had to think. 'Um —'

'I want someone like the heroes in the movies. A prince on a white horse who would whisk me away to his castle,' Brook started.

'Get real,' said Zahrah. 'You can't even ride a bike never mind a horse. You'd fall off the back. Sounds like you've watched too many Disney films, girl.'

'So? There's nothing wrong with having a dream.'

'OK,' said Leela. 'You don't have to say out loud what you want. Just write for a few moments.

'You sound like a teacher at exam time,' said Brook. 'No talking. No conferring.'

I didn't mind. I liked doing things like this. It was the sort of list that Erin and I used to write when I lived in Ireland. We were all quiet for a few minutes as we scribbled away.

'Right,' said Leela. 'Time's up. Brook, you go first.'

'OK. My perfect boy will be nice-looking, and sorry if that makes me shallow but I like beautiful things and beautiful people. It's because I'm a Pisces and we're romantic with high expectations.'

Zahrah sighed. 'Good-looking boys can be so dull, like they've never had to make any effort because people just fall at their feet.'

'Not so. Or else it would be the same for beautiful girls,' said Leela. 'And being one myself, I should know. No one could call me dull.'

I laughed but I got what Zahrah was saying. I'd briefly dated Callum Hesketh in September and he was the school boy-babe. It was true – he was totally in love with himself. Joe seemed to be the exception. He was good-looking but he didn't seem self-obsessed.

'So what else?' asked Leela.

'I think it's important that a boy is generous too,' said Brook. 'I hate tightness.'

'Yeah,' we all agreed.

'GSOH. Good sense of humour, very important,' said Brook, 'but someone who knows how to be romantic. I don't want some yob who treats me like a doormat and thinks that I am there to be his slave or bit of arm candy.'

Zahrah laughed. 'You are such a princess, Brook Holmes.'

'No I'm not. I just want to be treated well. I want the best.'

'Picasso said that women are either goddesses or doormats,' I said, remembering a line that I'd read about the famous artist who was apparently a bit of a lover boy himself.

'Then we must be goddesses,' said Leela. 'I don't want anyone wiping their feet on me.'

'Me neither,' said Zahrah.

'So what do you want then, Miss Picky?' Brook asked.

'God. Obvi, isn't it?' Zahrah shrugged. 'Someone I can have a decent conversation with – who has a brain.'

'Yeah, but if he's plug ugly I bet you wouldn't want to snog him,' said Brook.

'Beauty's only skin deep,' said Zahrah. 'Bet I *would* want to snog him if he was sensitive and intelligent.'

'OK. What about Tim Cole at school?' asked Leela. 'He's brainy and intelligent.'

Zahrah wrinkled her nose as if to say no thanks.

'See,' said Leela. 'You don't want to snog him because he's a geek.'

Zahrah rolled her eyes. 'No. It's not that. I don't want to snog him because there's no chemistry. And he only comes up to my knees! Give me a break.'

'What about you, India Jane? What's your perfect boy like?' asked Brook.

'Er . . .'

'Joe Donahue,' said Leela and sighed. 'And I don't blame you. He is lush.'

'Yeah,' said Brook dreamily. 'So what's happening there? You had the date at the art gallery, then what?'

'Zilch,' I said. 'Although he did hold my hand at the gallery but . . . it's his A-level year so maybe he's studying.'

Zahrah shook her head. 'Don't kid yourself, girl. He's a boy, isn't he? Believe me, if he's interested, he'll be in touch, even if he's in the middle of exams. And you've got your mock GCSEs coming up next term, but it hasn't put you off thinking about him.'

'Yeah,' I said.

'I disagree, Zahrah. That might be the case but maybe you have to help things along a little, India,' said Leela. 'Sometimes boys can be dopey when it comes to making a move and sometimes they can be plain lazy.'

'So what do you suggest?' I asked.

'You need a plan to get together with him. You could hang around outside his house and accidentally on purpose bump into him – like oh, Joe! I didn't know you lived around here.'

'Been there, done that when my mate Erin was over,' I said. 'I felt like a stalker when he caught us hanging around his house. I'm sure he knew what we were up to.'

'I think he should come to you. I don't think you should be making plans,' said Brook.

'God helps those who help themselves,' said Leela. 'So try something else, India. You're both in the scenery group, aren't you?'

I nodded. 'But it's sorted and everyone knows what they're doing.'

'Then you need to make an excuse to talk about some minor detail with him,' said Leela. 'Call him and ask for his advice. Boys love that. It makes them feel big and clever. 'Course they're not and we all know that but, hey, you have to play the game.'

Zahrah did one of her sucking air through her teeth noises. 'You girls. When are you going to get it? If it's meant to be with a boy, you don't have to play games. India, don't listen to them. If Joe's into you, he'll get in touch. That's how it is with boys. Really, *really*. Just be yourself and let him come to you.'

'Exactly,' said Brook.

Leela picked up a cushion from behind her head and chucked it at Zahrah. 'You think you're keeping it real. But, boy, if anyone's the romantic here, it's you. Boys aren't mind readers – they can't see what's in front of them. They *need* a helping hand.'

Zahrah shook her head. 'Not if it's real.'

'Have you got his number?' Leela asked.

I nodded. I had it on my phone and also in my memory.

'So call him,' she continued. 'Now.'

'Don't,' Zahrah cautioned.

'I think Zahrah's right,' I replied. 'I don't want to appear desperate. I don't think we're at that stage yet when I can call him like —'

'Make it happen,' said Leela.

23

'If you're the honey and he's the bee, he'll find you,' said Zahrah.

'What do you think, Brook?' I asked.

'Only you can decide,' she replied.

'Rubbish,' said Leela. 'Where's your phone?'

I pointed at my jacket. Leela got up from the bed and pulled out my phone, and stood over me until I dialled Joe's number. I prayed that he wasn't there – having a conversation with an audience of three listening in is not exactly in my comfort zone. Unluckily he was there and picked up.

'Hey India Jane.'

'Oh . . . Hi.'

Brook began swooning and clutching her heart. Leela started writhing about on the cushions as if she had ants in her pants. Zahrah looked at me with disapproval.

After a few moments' silence, Joe asked, 'So what can I do for you?'

'Yes. Oh. I need to talk through something about the scenery.'

'Oh yeah. Sorry about this morning had a . . . a thing to do. I heard it went well though. Tim called me. But you wanted to talk to me, OK, shoot.'

'Yes, I . . . er, need your advice about the opening night, er . . . run a few things past you seeing as I'm new to it and you've done it a few times before.'

Leela put her thumb and index finger together to form the sign of approval. Zahrah rolled her eyes up to the ceiling. Brook nodded and motioned in circles with her hand as if to say go on, go on.

'Oh. OK. When then? At school?'

'No, not at school,' I blurted as my mind did a quick scan of romantic places to meet in Notting Hill.

'OK. Not at school. How about next weekend then? Where? Shall I come to your place?'

'*Nooooo*. I mean . . . no, too many people. I mean . . . you know, family, they're very nosy. Our house is like a railway station at the weekend. Um. How about . . . er . . . how about . . . today at Ruby Red's café down near Portobello Road.'

'Today? When?'

'Um, later?' I said.

Leela looked shocked, shook her head and fell back against the cushions. I quickly realised that I sounded too eager. It was so hard getting the balance right. Cool, but not too cool. Interested but not over eager.

'I mean . . . not later today, I'm busy, oh yes, so busy busy busy like a bee that's me. I mean, how about . . . OK, tomorrow?'

'Can't do tomorrow,' said Joe. 'Family thing. But I could have done later today, shame . . .'

'No. OK. Today, I can probably get out of things. I could do um . . . er . . . f-f-four o'clock.' *Oh God, I just developed a stutter,* I thought.

'Done,' said Joe. 'See you there. I wanted to see you anyway.'

'Later,' I said and clicked off the phone. 'Done deal,' I said to my judges and jury.

Zahrah shook her head. '*Way* too easy.'

'You're the one who said not to play games,' said Leela. 'And she didn't.'

'And he said he wanted to see me anyway,' I said and punched the air. 'So, result.'

Brook looked thoughtful. 'Hmm. See how it goes. Least you *got* a result which is more than us three saddos.'

'Speak for yourself,' said Zahrah.

Chapter 3

The Nunnery Calls

I got to Ruby Red's ahead of time and went straight for the Ladies so that I could make any last minute repairs. Hair. Lip-gloss. Dab of cinnamon perfume.

When I walked back into the café, Joe had arrived and was sitting at a table in a quiet corner at the back. He was looking his usual handsome self in jeans and a blue fleece and he waved when he saw me.

I made my way over and as I got to him wondered how to greet him. Casual kiss on the cheek? Maybe. Hug? Too sisterly. Handshake? Definitely not. I sat down opposite and gave him a strange kind of salute which was like a hand flick.

'So. Hi,' I said.

He looked quizzically at my hand and then did the hand flick salute back. 'Yeah. Hi. So . . . what's up?'

'Next scenery meeting in two weeks' time. Can't do.'

Joe shrugged. 'OK. No prob. What you got on?'

'My grandmother's seventieth. Italy. All the family are going. Sorry to dump it all on you but there's no getting out of it.'

'Wow. Italy. Fab. No prob about the scenery though. It sounded like everyone loved the designs from what Tim said – lime, orange and bright pink, yeah? Great. And maybe we could put up some fairy lights to make it really magical and Bollywoodish. So most of it is sorted, yeah? Everyone seems to know what they're doing and it's ages until the show in December, so we're right on target. You could see everyone individually before you go if you wanted to check up on anything.'

'Yeah. But no need, um, as you say, everyone knows what they're doing. I . . . I just wanted to make sure that someone took the official meeting,' I said. He looked ill at ease. *It's obvious that this meeting is totally unnecessary,* I thought. *He's probably thinking that I am desperate. Oh God, I wish I hadn't arranged it.*

'No prob. Will do.' Joe jerked his chin at the counter. 'Want anything?'

Yeah, a snogathon somewhere cosy with you, I thought as I glanced at his gorgeous mouth and felt the rush of chemistry that I always did when I was with him, but I just nodded and said, 'Juice. Anything. Thanks.' I rummaged about in my pocket and found a few coins which I offered him. I wasn't sure of the etiquette. Should he pay? Should I pay? We weren't dating and, even if we were, I still wouldn't be sure what was what on the who pays front. I liked to think of myself as an independent type who would never rely on a boy to cough up for everything, but I'd read in a girls' mag that boys can feel emasculated if you come on too in control because sometimes they do like to pay. But, then again, I'd invited Joe to meet up and he was at school like me, not earning, and I knew his parents weren't loaded. What to do? How to be? It was *so* complicated.

Joe pushed my money back at me. 'On me,' he said gruffly.

I sat for a few minutes staring around the café, trying to look cool and alluring as he went and got the drinks. I needn't have bothered though as he didn't even glance in my direction when he queued up at the counter. An older man on the next table noticed me though. As he got up to leave, he glanced over and said, 'Cheer up, love. It might never happen.'

'Exactly,' I replied to him. 'It might not. That's exactly what I'm starting to think.'

The man shook his head, as if puzzled by what I'd said, then left the café. Moments later, Joe came back and put an apple juice in front of me. 'That OK?' he asked.

I nodded. 'Yes, thanks.'

'So?' Joe asked.

'Yes. So. Um, what you been doing today?'

'Coursework mainly. I've got a lot of catching up to do. You?'

'Same. Um. Er . . . I was round at Brook's. It was really funny because her mum was looking on a dating site and we all got talking about relationships and what we wanted and oh . . .' I hesitated for a moment and wondered if I'd totally said the

29

wrong thing and Mrs Holmes wouldn't appreciate me blabbing on about her search for a man to all and sundry. Maybe it was supposed to be top secret. 'Um. Maybe don't tell anyone that. I mean, some people don't like it made public that they're looking for relationships.'

Joe smiled for the first time that day. 'It's cool. I won't say anything. So, you got into a discussion. So what is it *you* want then, Miss Ruspoli?'

I shrugged and then before I could stop myself I blurted out Aunt Sarah's line. 'Buddha with balls and a Bentley.'

Joe almost spat his drink out. 'Pe*wffff*. Wow. You don't want much, do you? The Buddha, huh? Won't find many of them wandering round Notting Hill.'

'You know what I mean. Someone kind and sensitive and wise who isn't a wimp . . . I guess I don't mind about the Bentley.' I wondered whether to say a boy with a bike would do as Joe cycles to school but somehow, the mood didn't seem right for flirting.

Joe nodded. 'Wise but not a wimp. Yeah. Won't find many of *them* wandering around Notting Hill either.'

'Got to aim high. Why? What do you want?'

Joe seemed to visibly relax as if he was glad I'd asked him. 'Good question. What do I want? Well, that's just it. I really don't know. Early days.' He glanced around the café. 'I guess I want the chance to play the field a bit, sample all that's on offer so that, when I do "go steady" or whatever, I'm not going to want out after a few weeks.'

I felt my heart sink. He'd talked like this before. When I'd first met him in Greece and also just before our first kiss at the Bollywood party at Leela's. He said he'd liked me then but didn't want to mess me around, partly because he didn't want to be a rat, partly because he didn't want to hurt me and partly because his mum and my aunt Sarah were best mates and he didn't want to have them on his case.

I decided to be brave. 'So . . . how does all that relate to us?'

Joe flinched. I immediately regretted asking him because I know that boys hate to be confronted about their feelings. Even my mum jokes that the four words my dad hates the most are, 'We need to talk'.

'Look, India Jane . . .' he started. I felt my heart sink further. 'There is no us.' He must have seen my face fall. I've never been good at keeping my feelings hidden. 'Look, I really do like you, just . . . I've told you before. I don't want to commit at the moment. It's not you . . .'

'Yeah, it's not you, it's me. Nothing personal. You just want to be friends.'

Joe sighed heavily. *He and Zahrah would make a great pair,* I thought. *They seem to speak the same language.* 'Look. I see relationships as being like a train, you get one compartment at a time – not the whole lot straight off, it has to build.'

'So let's let it build then,' I said and smiled as if to say I could be light and casual. 'Let's play builders. You can be Bob the Builder.'

Joe half smiled. 'Too late for that.'

'Why?' I asked and immediately regretted it. *Shut up now India,* I thought. *You're beginning to sound desperate.*

'Just, well . . . remember I said about not committing? Well we haven't, have we? I mean, we're not a *we*, are we?'

'No. 'Course not.'

'Good,' he said, 'because I don't want you to think that I've let you down, but I've got to tell you this. I . . . I . . . I've started hanging out with someone. I've known her for a while so it's not new really. Nothing serious. I met her last year and . . . well . . . see, she has the same attitude to relationships as me, that it's, er . . . for fun. I was going to tell you, India, honestly I was, because I know, least I kind of know, that you were hoping that something was going to happen with us and, as I said, I don't want to start something then let you down. And it's important to me that you hear it from me after what happened with Mia. I didn't want that to happen again.'

I felt like he'd stuck a knife in my heart. 'That's big of you,' I said and immediately regretted it because I knew that I sounded bitter. When I started school after I'd met Joe in Greece, I found out a small fact that he'd forgotten to tell me – and that was that he had a girlfriend called Mia.

'I just want things to be clear between us and I want us to be —'

'Friends,' I finished for him.

Joe looked around the café as if he'd rather be anywhere but there. 'You know that I rate you, India Jane. I think you're a great girl just . . . I don't feel comfortable dating someone so close to home in case things don't work out and you got hurt.'

'Yeah, you said. But what if I'd dumped you first?'

'I'd say that I probably asked for it,' said Joe. 'You deserve someone who doesn't mess you around.'

'I don't see why you can't be that person.'

Joe smiled sadly and reached out and put his hand over mine. 'Maybe later. When we're away from . . . oh you know.'

I pulled my hand out from under his and got up. 'I was only kidding,' I said. 'Don't worry about me. I only wanted to see if you could be there for the scenery team while I'm away really, to get the designs in motion, so that's cool. I didn't mean the other stuff about us. As you say, there is no us. I was just messing about. Teasing.'

'Yeah. 'Course. Cool,' said Joe.

'Yeah,' I said.

We both knew I was lying. When I left the café, I felt tears prick the back of my eyes. *I hate boys*, I thought as I stomped back out into the dark wet afternoon. *I hate Joe. And I'm going to be a nun.*

Chapter 4

The Challenge

'No way,' said Leela when I told her my plan on Monday as we gathered around the radiators outside the sports hall in break.

'I'm serious. I'm off boys for good. They do my head in,' I said.

'Not all boys,' said Brook. 'Just Joe Donahue. There will be someone else much nicer than him out there.'

'Yeah, he was the wrong boy for you,' said Leela.

'I think you're being very sensible,' said Zahrah. 'Just forget about him and boys in general.'

'*No*,' Leela objected. 'Come on, guys. It's the beginning of November. The skies are grey. It's ages before Christmas comes along to cheer us up. You have to drop the defeatist attitude.'

'Christmas might be a way away but we still have bonfire parties we could go to this week,' said Brook.

I shook my head. 'I am going to be a recluse,' I said.

'No!' said Leela. 'I forbid it! What you need, in fact, what we all need is a challenge. And . . . I have just the one.'

Zahrah rolled her eyes. 'Oh no, here we go,' she said.

'Cool,' said Brook and did a low bow. 'Speak forth, O my captain, for I will do thy bidding.'

'OK, so get ready. It's about seven weeks until the end of term so . . . the challenge is that we all have to get a boyfriend – and I mean a *proper* boyfriend – before then.'

'Not me,' said Zahrah. 'Not interested.'

'Nor me,' I said and joined my hands as if in prayer. 'I am now Sister Mary Consuela Bernadette India. No boys allowed.'

'Chickens,' said Leela and she put her hands under her armpits, stuck her elbows out at an angle and started making clucking noises. Brook did the same. *If you can't beat them, join them*, I thought and did the same and added a bit of pecking motion and clucking for further effect.

Of course that had to be the moment that Joe went past and he was with Callum Hesketh, the school babe who I'd dated briefly in the first part of term.

Joe cracked up. 'Nice one, India.'

Callum stood for a moment with a hand on his hip and surveyed us. 'Er yeah, do the funky chicken, girls,' he said.

I immediately straightened up and tried to look cool. Too late. They'd moved on and disappeared around a corner.

'Ah well, at least he'll remember me as being different,' I said.

Leela linked her arm through mine. 'Forget him. He's so not

worth it. So ze challenge. It will be so good for us. Boost our confidence. Who's in?'

'Maybe,' said Brook.

'Not me,' said Zahrah.

I laughed. 'Doesn't that just sum up our attitudes to life? Leela's a yes yes yes. Brook's a maybe, let me think about it and Zahrah's a no.'

Zahrah stuck out her bottom lip. 'That makes me sound negative and I'm not,' she said. 'Just Leela's always got a plan and most of them are mad. You don't know her as well as Brook and I do. Stick around a few more months and you'll be plugging your ears when she announces that she's got a plan!'

I squeezed her arm. 'Sorry Zahrah, I didn't mean to insinuate that you're negative. I know you're not.'

'Sensible is the word you were looking for,' said Zahrah. 'One of us has to be. Like Brook and Leela have got their heads in the clouds about a lot of things, whereas I have my feet firmly on the ground. But what about you? Are you in with Leela's latest?'

'I don't know,' I said. 'I don't think that you can force love or put a deadline on it. It's either going to happen or not.'

'It doesn't have to be *love*,' said Leela. 'Just a boyfriend.'

'You said a proper boyfriend,' I said.

'Yeah. And what's a proper boyfriend anyway?' asked Zahrah. 'Define.'

'Yeah,' said Brook. 'Do you mean someone you're actually dating or do you mean kissing with tongues?'

'Both,' said Leela. 'Er . . . basically someone who phones you back if you call them and someone you don't feel weird about calling in the first place and who actually turns up if you have a date.'

'And what if we fail?' I asked.

Leela grinned. 'Aha. So a flicker of interest then, eh?'

'Oh, let's go for it,' said Brook. 'It will be a laugh. And I've already got a few contenders in mind.'

'Who?' I asked.

'A boy who lives on our street. Liam Wiseman. Doesn't go to our school. And Mark Mitchell from the Sixth Form.'

Leela nodded. 'Yeah. Mark's nice but you can only have one.'

'So there are rules now are there, Miss Bossy Boots?' asked Zahrah.

'Not really but he wouldn't be a proper boyfriend if you were seeing someone else, would he?' Leela replied.

'I guess,' said Zahrah.

'What about you, Leela?' I asked. 'Got anyone in mind?'

Leela looked coy but was saved from replying as the bell for the end of break shrilled behind us, and pupils began to swarm up and down the corridors heading for their next class. Ours was double English and we were having a treat. We were doing Shakespeare's *Romeo and Juliet* as part of our coursework and our teacher Mr Pacey had arranged for us to see the film version of the play directed by Baz Luhrmann and starring Leonardo Di Caprio.

'It's soooo romantic,' sighed Brook when the movie got to the part where Romeo gatecrashes Juliet's family party and they see each other for the first time and zing ping go their heartstrings.

'It is at first,' whispered Zahrah. 'And then . . .' She acted out someone having their throat cut.

'Shhh at the back,' said Mr Pacey.

As I sat and watched the star-crossed lovers go through their series of mix-ups and miscommunications on the screen, part of my mind started to drift away. *There's no getting away from it*, I thought. *Love is a tragedy and I am a tragic heroine*. I started imagining a series of paintings I could do for my art project. Mr Bailey, our teacher, had asked us to paint a series of self-portraits and I thought it would be good to do some like the Pre-Raphaelite painters who were big on tragic heroines. Millais, Burne-Jones, Rossetti – they had all painted beautiful women with a distant look of sadness in their eyes, as if they had been let down big time by love. One of the most famous was of Ophelia. Millais's painting shows her lying in the river covered in flowers after she drowned because Hamlet had driven her mental. *Is that how I'm going to end up*? I wondered. *Floating in the Thames with a poetry book in my hand, flowers in my hair and a tattoo with Joe's name engraved on my arm so everyone can see who has done me wrong.* I could see the painting in my mind's eye. People would come from far and wide, look at it, feel sadness and ask, Who was that poor girl? I sat back in my chair, assumed a tragic heroine's pose (wistful expression that hints of sorrows untold, a slight weariness around the shoulders and limp wrists) and watched the film. I felt a bond with all the women through the ages who had been let down by love. Zahrah passed along some mints at one point and I wondered if she had noticed my pose, but she didn't comment. Clearly it was lost on her.

As the film continued, I found myself starting to get cross. Romeo was acting like a total love rat, in love with some girl called Rosaline at the beginning of the play and then changing his mind in a flash as soon as he meets Juliet. *What happened to Rosaline?* I thought. *That's what I'd like to know. Poor girl. Romeo is clearly nothing more than another stupid boy with a phobia about commitment who can't make up his mind who or what he wants. Like Joe.* I started wondering why I am attracted to boys like Joe who make me feel uncomfortable or don't want to commit. *Love is a funny thing,* I thought. Then I remembered that I wasn't in love with Joe any more. And then I felt even crosser. With him and myself. Blimey. *No wonder those tragic heroines look so miserable,* I thought. *Love is rubbish.*

I made myself focus back on the movie. The scene where Romeo spends the night in Juliet's room. Quite sweet actually but then he's off. Gone with the larks or was it the nightingales? Whichever.

Brook, Leela and even Zahrah looked spellbound by the film. I watched them for a few moments. I couldn't imagine any of them drowning themselves over a stupid boy. *Nor me,* I thought. *Times have changed since Romeo and Jules's day. We don't have to let boys play the tune, with us just dancing along and letting them lead until they break our hearts. No. Ours is the age of girl power. I don't want to be sad or a tragic heroine. I want to be like Aunt Sarah. Her husband, who was the great love of her life, left her and did she lose her mind or wither away and become a shadow of her former self? No. She became a businesswoman, earned a ton of dosh and showed him she didn't need him. Although sometimes I see a hint of sadness in her eyes, she doesn't wallow in it. No. She kicks butt. She's a butt-kicking heroine. I want to be like her, but . . . I don't want to give up on love either. Not yet and especially not because of Joe Donahue. I want to meet a boy who doesn't do my head in. A boy who is kind and sensitive and, most of all, likes me – adores me. And what's more . . . I am going to find him.*

While up on the screen, Romeo drank the potion and ranted on about it having touched Juliet's lips, I thought, *Oh grow up, you stupid prat, for heaven's sake, you've only known Juliet five minutes.* I leaned over and poked Leela. 'Lee,' I whispered.

'What?'

'The challenge. I'm in.' Then I made a fist. 'Girl power.'

Leela gave me a strange look but did the fist back. 'Um. Yeah. OK. Girl power.'

I settled back to watch the end of the movie and felt determined that I would find a boy. A nice boy. A gorgissimus boy. No compromises. An equal. Maybe even The One. *So look out London boys*, I thought. *Here I come. And Joe stupoid Donahue. You, my friend, are history.*

Chapter 5

Romeo, Romeo, Where4 Art Thou Romeo?

We fell into a fun routine – after school every night, we'd take it in turns to pick a location then go boy spotting. By the end of week one, we'd hung out in all the local cafés that were popular with schools in our area, we'd mooched about outside two boys' schools as well as outside the local cinema. On Friday, Leela dragged us along to a bonfire party in the local park, but it was pouring with rain so the fireworks got cancelled and the bonfire was a big wet mass of wood. Leela wanted to stay because there did seem to be a lot of boys around but, after we got drenched in a torrential downpour, Zahrah called a halt to the venture.

'We look like a bunch of sad stalkers,' she said as we adjourned with dripping wet hair and coats to Starbucks to dry off.

'Seek and ye shall find,' said Brook.

'Er . . . I think you might find that is a quote by Jesus and he's talking about finding the kingdom of heaven, not boys,' said Zahrah with a frown. She knew her Bible well on account of her family being devout Christians.

'Whatever,' said Brook, leading us to our favourite place by the window. 'The principle applies whatever you're looking for. Like, you're not going to meet anyone if you stay at home and don't get out, right?'

'Not unless you have a bunch of older brothers who all have gorgeous friends,' said Leela.

'Ranjiv is cute,' said Brook, looking wistfully at Leela.

'Don't even go there,' she said. 'He's taken. Hate to tell you but he's all loved up at the moment. Girl called Chloe. Don't know what she sees in him myself.'

'Oh I do,' I said, and then blushed as Zahrah, Leela and Brook all turned to stare at me. 'He's very handsome, Leela. All your family are gorgeous like Bollywood actors.' I'd met Leela's mum and dad a couple of times when I'd been over to their house. Her mum was stunning. Leela told me that when she was younger she had been a contestant in a Miss India competition and the judges wanted to put her through for the Miss World contest, but she decided to go and train as a pharmacist instead.

'Try living with them,' said Leela.

Brook sighed. 'The tragedy of my life is that Ranjiv only sees me as Leela's silly little friend.'

'Maybe that's because you go stupid whenever he's around,' retorted Leela.

Brook gave her a look of disdain. 'I do not do stupid,' she said. 'I am way too cool for that. I just go, um . . . quiet.'

'Stupid,' said Leela with a wicked grin.

'I go stupid with some boys,' I confessed. 'Like I can be myself with the ones I don't care about but, if I fancy someone, I start talking hogwash and blushing and I've even been known to knock things over.'

'I thought you only had eyes for Joe Donahue, India,' said Zahrah.

'That was then and it never meant that I couldn't appreciate a cute boy like Ranjiv – although it was Erin who really fancied him. Sorry Brook – but I wouldn't worry about us because I reckon Ireland is a bit far away, and he's not really my type.'

'So what is your type?' asked Leela.

'Not sure yet. I'll think about it and get back to you.'

Leela and Brook went off to get the drinks while Zahrah and I settled down on the sofas.

'So Leela,' said Brook when they came back with the drinks, and also Mikey who is in our year at school, 'where exactly are we supposed to meet these perfect boys? So far, it's been hopeless. A dead loss.'

'Perfect boys? Talking about me again. What's all this?' asked Mikey. He was a new friend of mine who lived near Aunt Sarah's house and we often walked to and from school together.

He kept saying that he wanted to be more than a mate one day, but I'd told him that it was never going to happen. I didn't fancy him. It wasn't that he wasn't cute; he was. With his dark floppy hair and big brown eyes, he was very sweet but just not right for me – too young-looking. I like hanging out with him though – he is a laugh.

Leela quickly filled him in on the quest.

'Interesting,' he said. 'Well of course I would offer myself but then I am taken at the moment.' He had been dating Amy in our French class since just before half-term.

'Shame,' said Zahrah and we laughed because Zahrah and Mikey would have made a totally unlikely couple. She would have made mincemeat of him.

'So where are we going to meet new boys, Leela?' I asked.

'Early days still,' she replied. 'But I think we should try a new tactic.'

Zahrah groaned.

'No, wait, let's hear her out,' said Brook. 'I feel a plan is coming upon our small but perfectly formed friend.'

'Oi. Less of the small. I'm five foot, if you don't mind. And yes, I do have a plan. Tomorrow afternoon, Portobello Road. There are always loads of boys from all over London and even some from Europe.'

'That's true,' said Brook. 'Good idea, Leela.'

'Has she hypnotised you or something?' Zahrah asked.

Brook shook her head. 'No.' And then she made her face go completely deadpan and spoke in a robotic way. 'Although I will obey. I will obey.' She relaxed her face. 'At least she comes up with ideas.'

'Yeah but there's a slight flaw in the plan, like it's not much good if you fall in love with a German or Italian boy. Long-distance love never works,' said Zahrah.

'And how are we going to get to meet them?' I asked. 'This hanging about looking cool and interesting hasn't exactly worked for us. We've seen a few decent boys but they've just walked straight past. We need some excuse to talk to them.'

'Exactly,' said Brook. 'India's right, we need some reason to talk to them and boys don't always like it if you make the first move.'

'Oh. Mikey. You're a boy —' Leela started.

Mikey lifted his right arm and pumped his muscle. 'So you'd noticed,' he said in a silly deep voice.

'Only just,' said Zahrah. Mikey playfully punched her.

'What should we do?' Leela continued.

Mikey thought for a few moments then grinned. 'I know. What you need is an opening, so why not pretend that you're doing research for a project about what boys want from girls. You could say that you're doing it for the school magazine. You could even submit it to the school magazine – I bet everyone would want to read the results, wouldn't they?'

'Mikey my man, you are awesome,' said Brook 'That is a brilliant idea.'

Mikey looked very pleased with himself.

'So who's in?' Leela asked. 'Tomorrow, turn up looking sharp with a notepad and paper.'

'I'm in,' I said. 'Sounds like a laugh.'

'Me too,' said Brook.

'And me too, I guess. Someone has to come along to make sure that you don't get arrested,' said Zahrah.

'Excellent,' said Leela.

'Now, questions,' said Mikey. 'You each need to think up three or four so you look professional.'

'Yes, good idea,' said Leela. 'OK girls. Have a think then email what you come up with to me when you get home and I'll print them out ready for tomorrow.'

Brook saluted. 'Yes, sir.'

Mikey got up to go. 'I have to go in a minute but . . .'

'OK. Bye and thanks for your great idea,' said Leela.

'Anytime,' said Mikey, 'but . . .' He shifted about on his feet for a few seconds and looked awkward.

'Spill,' said Zahrah. 'What is it you want?'

Mikey coughed. 'Um. Advice.'

'Sure,' said Zahrah. 'What is it you want to know?'

Mikey sat down again, leaned towards us and said in a whisper. 'I . . . I want to know how to be a good kisser.'

'Why? Do you think you're not?' asked Brook.

'That's it. I don't know. I mean, Amy has never complained or anything but . . . I'd like to be more confident about it and . . . well, there are four of you.'

'Yes. Four of us. And?' asked Brook.

'Um. I wonder if you'd show me.'

'Show you or tell you?' I asked.

Mikey's expression grew cheeky and he looked at me hopefully. 'Both?'

I looked at Brook, Leela and Zahrah. None of them said anything. Brook shrugged her shoulders.

'We'll discuss it,' I said. 'And get back to you later.'

'How about on my birthday? Mum said I could have a party – which you're all invited to, of course.'

'Consider it our birthday present,' said Brook.

Mikey's face lit up. 'Really? Cool,' he said, and headed for the door.

'So?' asked Zahrah.

Brook shrugged. 'We could show him. I don't mind. He's a nice guy and sometimes I feel for boys, like, where are they supposed to learn if we don't show them.'

'I guess,' I said. 'But I'm not kissing him. I don't mind giving him a few pointers though.'

'How do you know that you're a good kisser?' asked Zahrah.

'Experience,' I said. 'Erin and I sold kisses at a Christmas fête one year over in Ireland. It was hysterical. By the end of the day, I had really got the hang of the fact that there are all sorts of kisses: light, deep, sloppy, dry.'

'And how do you know you're a good kisser?' asked Zahrah turning to Brook.

Brook sat up with her back very straight. 'It's just something I was born with.' She ran her hands over her body. 'This bod was made for love,' she drawled in a Texan accent. 'And I was born to kiss and be kissed.'

Zahrah rolled her eyes. 'Oh for God's sake.'

Brook laughed. 'I've practised,' she said. 'There's always some boy like Mikey who wants to learn. And I've done my homework. I've read up on it and then practised.'

'Good. So you can teach Mikey. Sorted,' said Leela.

'What about you, Lee?' I asked.

Leela blushed. 'OK. I haven't snogged many boys but I think I'm OK at it. I've had no complaints.' She cleared her throat. 'And in the meantime, let's do a list of the boy contenders so far. Zahrah. You go first.'

'No one.'

'Oh come on, there must be someone at school you fancy a little.'

Zahrah looked pensive. 'OK,' she said after a few moments. 'I guess there is Mr Bailey.'

'Ewww,' Leela and Brook chorused.

'You can't have him – he's a teacher,' said Leela.

'And he so fancies himself,' said Brook.

'You're always making up rules,' said Zahrah. 'You asked my opinion and that's it.'

Leela wrote down Mr Bailey. 'OK. I'll add his name but we all know he's not a real contender.'

Zahrah shrugged. 'There's no one else I fancy.'

'Joe Donahue for India, although he's out of bounds now,' said Brook, 'Callum Hesketh, Mark Mitchell.'

'Callum Hesketh is a waste of time,' I said. 'And he's already in a relationship.'

'Who with?' asked Brook.

'Himself.'

'OK,' said Leela and she crossed Callum's name off. 'Er . . . Liam Wiseman, Ramesh from the drama group . . . You got any to add, India?' she asked.

I shook my head. 'Eddie O'Neil from the Sixth Form fancies me, but it's not mutual,' I said. Eddie was OK but there wasn't any chemistry. I wondered if I'd ever feel as strongly about another boy as I had about Joe. He really had got to me and I still felt cut up about it. *What's the point,* I thought.

Leela lightly slapped my arm. 'Enough of the glum face,' she said. 'It's too early to give up.' She did the girl power fist.

'You're right,' I said and did the fist back at her, but I wasn't feeling very enthusiastic about it. *Maybe you only ever get one true love in a lifetime,* I thought. *Joe was mine and, from now on, all will be compromise.*

I could feel the nunnery beckoning again.

Chapter 6

Cut up

'What are you doing, India?' asked my younger brother Dylan later that night as he watched me cut out bits of girls' heads and bodies from magazines and spread them over the kitchen table. 'Is this some kind of witchcraft ritual?'

'No,' I said as I continued snipping. 'I'm making a collage for art.' I took the eyes from one girl, the hair from another, the chin from another and stuck them down on a piece of paper. 'I've had a new idea for my project of self-portraits. I am going to call this one *Cut Up*.' *Cut up was how I felt after Joe had told me that he was seeing someone else,* I thought, snipping off a leg and sticking it down, *so it will be a perfect self-portrait to do to represent my state of mind.* Mr Bailey, the art teacher, was going to think I was totally mental when he saw my latest batch of work. Tragic heroines. Cut-up girl collages. And then I wondered if Joe might see them – art is one of his subjects. *I hope he does*, I thought. *Then he'll see how he's made me feel!*

'She looks like a freak to me,' said Dylan. He looked over my shoulder at my collage then went to the fridge and helped himself to juice and a slice of carrot cake. 'Want anything?'

'No thanks,' I said. We'd just had dinner so I wasn't hungry any more and I was enjoying creating my cut-up self while I thought about my questions for Leela's survey. I found art could be very therapeutic some days – it let me express feelings that sometimes I found hard to put into words.

'What do you want from a girl?' I asked Dylan as he sat down opposite me and began to cram cake in his mouth.

'Nothing,' he said. 'I don't like girls. They always want to kiss me.'

I should have known better than to ask a twelve-year-old, although, judging by the number of calls he got, girls weren't put off by the fact that he wasn't interested. Dylan is very good-looking with the same fine features as Mum – cherub-faced with long eyelashes and red blond hair. He'll be a heartbreaker by the time he's fifteen. As I sat there cutting and gluing, various members of the family came into the kitchen, including Lewis who is a student in his first year at university. He has digs in Crouch End but comes home a couple of times a week to eat and get his laundry done. Like my other brother, Ethan, Lewis has my dad's dark Italian looks – they're handsome too, but in a different way to Dylan.

As always in the mad house I live in, my business was soon

everyone's business and I began to wish that I had started my collage in the privacy of my room upstairs. Dad came and sat at the top of the table and started making a collage of his own. Kate sauntered in with her red silk Chinese dressing gown on and her long dark hair freshly washed and smelling of the peach shampoo in the bathroom. She sat down and had a look at what I was doing.

'I think you may be in need of a shrink,' she pronounced before getting up and disappearing for the rest of the evening. (We don't see a lot of her these days. She's more like a lodger than a cousin whose house we're living in.)

Mum made everyone hot chocolates and Lewis and Dylan sat and stuffed their faces with choc chip biscuits. What those boys can put away is breathtaking.

'What's your perfect girl, Lewis?' I asked.

'The perfect girl kisses you goodnight then turns into a pizza,' said Lewis. Everyone groaned. It was a very old joke. 'Why?'

'I'm trying to work out what I want from the perfect boy,' I replied.

'I wouldn't worry,' said Mum. 'You're young. You'll get to know lots of boys and discover what you want along the way.'

I looked at the strange creature I had created on paper in front of me. I hoped that I never really ended up being so torn apart and I made myself remember my resolve not to go under because of a boy. *Be positive*, I told myself as I put the collage to one side.

'We're doing a . . . um . . . project survey sort of thing,' I said.
'I need some questions to ask boys about what they want from
girls. Any ideas. Dad? Lewis? Dylan?'

They all replied at once. My family is anything but shy.

'Her phone number,' said Lewis.

'Love, loyalty, good times,' said Dad with an affectionate
glance at Mum.

'To get off my case and leave me alone,' said Dylan.

'I don't want to know what *you* want,' I said. 'I need questions
to ask boys tomorrow.'

'OK. Ask what puts them off a girl,' said Dylan.

'Good one,' I said and wrote it down.

'What would impress you if a girl did it?' said Lewis.

'What makes a good kisser?' said Dad.

'Excellent,' I said and scribbled them down too.

'Describe what you want from a relationship,' said Mum.

'Thanks,' I said and wrote that down too. It was a good start
and Leela would be pleased.

When everyone had gone to bed or, in Lewis's case, gone home,
I went up to my room and was about to go to bed myself when
the phone rang. I quickly picked it up before it woke everyone
up.

It was Erin. 'India, thank God – I'm so glad you're there.'

She sounded weird, slightly out of breath.

'Why?' I asked. 'What's going on? Are you OK?'

'Me yeah. Sort of. I just got back from Shawn Casey's house.

It was his birthday and oh . . . Jesus, what a nightmare.'

'Nightmare? Why? What happened?'

'Scott.'

'What about Scott?'

At that moment, Dad put his head around my door. 'Who is it?'

'For me,' I said. 'Erin.'

'Bit late to be calling,' said Dad.

I nodded and luckily he disappeared. 'Sorry Erin, parent patrol. You were saying . . . about Scott?'

'Yeah. Sorry to be calling late. I just needed to talk to you. He's out of control, India. I don't know what to do.'

'Why? What happened?'

'Remember I told you that he'd got into drinking a lot and smoking.'

'Yeah but he's always been a bit like that, hasn't he?'

'It's getting worse. I'm so worried about him.'

'Why? What exactly has he been doing?'

'He's using skunk. I know he's smoked grass before, I've seen him do it loads of times – but this is much stronger stuff and it's like he has a total personality change when he smokes it.'

'Like how?'

'He turns horrible, loud and aggressive. And sarcastic, really mean to people. Not the Scott I know at all. Like at the party, he turned up about nine, stoned – he looked totally out of it, his eyes bloodshot and blurry. Shawn didn't look happy that he was there. I said I'd look after him and Scott heard me. He turned on me and started taunting me in a lispy little girl's voice saying, "Erin Werin, gonna look after me". Then he almost fell over. I leaned in quickly to catch him before he crashed into something and he pushed me against a wall and tried to snog me, but it was awful, slobbery and heavy and I know Scott is a good kisser, least he is when he's not stoned. Shawn saw that I was trying to shove him off and stepped in and Scott went for him. A couple of Shawn's mates threw him out, and I am so worried about him – like where did he go? And in that state? I want to call his house, but I don't want to get his parents involved.'

'Have you tried his mobile?'

'Tried that first. No reply. I don't know what I should do, like stay out of it or try and talk to him.

'Oh God, poor you. That's a really hard one. Look it's late. There's nothing you can do now; he probably staggered home and is snuggled up in bed oblivious to it all. Leave it for now and see how he is next time you see him. Or call him tomorrow.'

'I guess. Oh hell. I'm worried he's going to do something and regret it. What would you do?'

'I think I'd probably try to talk to him when he's not been smoking but, with guys like that, they can get defensive and accuse you of sounding like a teacher or a Miss Goody-Two-Shoes. It's not going to be an easy conversation.'

'I know. He's already said that I'm no fun because I don't want to try smoking it but I really don't want to. I've seen how

55

people change when they do. It really isn't like grass. It's like they get zombified.'

'What do your mates say?'

'To keep away from him but, India, we go back a long way and I know that he's a nice guy underneath. I don't want to see him get into trouble.'

'Then talk to him.'

'Yeah. No. Oh God. I'll try. Not easy. How are you?'

I decided that this wasn't the time to drone on about my tragic love life. 'Fine. Nothing major to report. Listen, try and get a good night's kip and keep me informed. Anytime you need to talk, yeah?'

'Yeah. Thanks, India Jane. I miss you.'

'I miss you too.'

'Laters.'

I glanced at the photo by my bed of Erin and me. Both pulling daft faces for the camera. I felt bad for her. She'd sounded so anxious. She'd been really into Scott last year. I knew him too when I was in Ireland. He was a cutenick with a cheeky grin that could melt most people – teachers and girls. I tried to imagine how it would be if Joe was in trouble. I think, like Erin, I'd feel I had to do something. I couldn't just stand back and watch him fall apart in front of me. Sometimes it was hard not living near to Erin any more. Even though I had new mates, Erin would always be my best friend and, when she was sad, I felt it too. *Some days feel all out of sync,* I thought. I got changed for bed then snuggled down under the duvet. *PoorScott. Poor Erin.*

Chapter 7

The Survey

'If he mirrors what you're doing, he's interested,' Brook read out of a manual about body language in the self-help department of the bookshop near Portobello Road.

'So if you stand on your head and he stands on his, he's interested?' asked Leela.

Brook slapped her arm lightly. 'Since when has standing on your head been a way to attract boys?'

'Since junior school when showing off her knickers was her favourite party trick,' said Zahrah.

'Hmm. Probably not the best technique any more,' I said, 'although worth a try if nothing else works.'

Leela laughed. 'I did not show off my knickers. Give me a break.'

Zahrah raised an eyebrow. *It must be nice for these guys*, I thought, *they've hung out together for years*. I felt envious. My family had been on the move my whole life and I'd always felt that, as soon as I'd made friends, I was saying goodbye to them. Hopefully, this time, we'd be staying in Notting Hill at least until I'd finished school. I couldn't bear another move and having to start all over again.

'OK, team,' said Brook. 'Ready to go and stop some boys' hearts?'

I shook my head. I felt underdressed and a bit scruffy in my jeans, sneakers, padded jacket and striped scarf. I'd dressed for the weather, which was cold and threatening rain, rather than to look the part of a professional interviewer. Brook had borrowed her mum's trench coat and was wearing a red beret to match her red lipstick. She looked amazing. Really grown-up and self-assured. Leela also looked smart in a knee-length grey coat and fab black riding boots. At least Zahrah was also in jeans.

Leela peered out of the window at the busy street. She had brought us all a clipboard so that we looked the part and handed one to each of us. 'You'll be fine, India,' she said. 'Let's go.'

Leela and Brook were straight in interviewing and flirting, while Zahrah and I stood back and watched for a while. I think Zahrah was feeling as reluctant about the whole venture as I was. A lady who knew Zahrah's mum walked past and she got involved in a conversation with her. Across the street, Leela motioned that I should approach a couple of boys who were standing close by looking at a stall that sold CDs.

I took a deep breath and approached the boys, one of whom was tall and dark, the other had a stockier build like he played rugby. 'Er . . . excuse me. Do you mind if I ask you a few questions for a survey?'

'What sort of survey?' asked the dark-haired boy.

'About what boys want from girls.'

The boy's face lit up. 'Hmm. What do you think, Josh?' he asked his mate. 'What do we want from girls?'

His friend put the palms of his hands up to the level of my chest and made a jiggly motion like he was about to grab my breasts. 'Sex,' he said.

I took a step away. 'And . . . and what turns you off about girls?'

'Girls who don't want sex,' said his mate and they both laughed like they'd made the best joke ever.

'And your perfect girl? In fact don't bother. I think I know the answer. Thanks very much; you've been very helpful,' I blurted, stepping even further back.

The dark boy shrugged. 'You did ask. Now let me ask you something for a survey I'm doing. Any chance of us doing it?'

His friend cracked up again and I realised that I was wasting my time with them. I moved back to join Zahrah, who was still talking to her mum's friend. *Maybe it would be better to ask a boy who is on his own*, I thought. *Sometimes, when there's a bunch of them, they act a lot cockier than they actually are.* I watched the passers-by for a while and then I spotted a boy who appeared

59

to be alone. As he approached, I took a few steps towards him. He was small with a sweet mouse-like face.

'Excuse me,' I started.

The boy looked terrified and turned his face away.

'I just want to ask you a few questions,' I said as he hurried by. He didn't look back. *Hmm*, I thought, *my interviewing technique clearly needs some work.*

Not long after, another boy approached. He had an open friendly face and shoulder-length curly hair. I walked towards him with a smile. 'Hi. I'm doing a survey to discover what boys want from girls,' I said again.

The boy stopped and looked me up and down. 'Hmm. What do I want from a girl?'

I smiled again to encourage him in case he was shy. 'Yes.'

He nodded and looked pensive for a few moments. 'Right. Three things. Great boobs. Great bum. Total subservience.'

'Oh. I . . . And . . . um, I am sure you'll make someone very happy one day,' I said as I hastened over the road and said, 'Not,' under my breath.

'What is it with these stupid boys?' I asked Zahrah, who was now on her own again. I quickly filled her in on the answers that I'd been given and she burst out laughing.

'Let me have a go,' she said and darted out in front of a small boy who was strolling past.

'Hey you,' she said. 'I'm doing a survey.'

The boy stopped and looked at Zahrah as if she was going to attack him. I thought he was going to hurry on like the other boy had but he stayed put. 'OK,' he squeaked.

'So. How do you know if a girl is The One?' asked Zahrah.

'The One?'

'Yeah.'

'The one what?'

'The One as in your soulmate, love of your life, you know, *The One*,' Zahrah expanded.

'I'm only thirteen,' said the boy. 'I don't even know what a soulmate is.'

'Your other half. Someone you love more than anyone else in the world, right?'

'OK,' said the boy, but he looked completely puzzled. 'I love my dog Petra best in the world.'

Zahrah wasn't put off. 'No. I'm talking human. Soulmate. If you did meet her, what qualities would she have?'

Fur and four paws in his case, I thought. I felt myself getting the giggles. *Zahrah's technique needs more work than mine, although she might be good at interviewing those politicians you see on telly sometimes who sidestep awkward questions.*

'Well?' Zahrah insisted.

'Er . . . she'd have a nice smile.'

'And . . .'

'Um . . . she could, er . . . do party tricks . . .'

'Party tricks?'

'Yeah. Like lick her eyebrows. Yeah, I'd like a girl who could do that. That would be cool.'

Zahrah gave the poor boy one of her withering looks (raised

eyebrow and an expression that says, Are you for real?) 'Thanks. And I sincerely hope you find what you're looking for.'

'Can I go now?' asked the boy.

Zahrah waved him away and he scuttled off down the street. I creased up laughing.

'What's so funny?' asked Zahrah.

'You are. In fact, not funny, terrifying. He was so sweet.'

Zahrah shrugged. 'You were right about one thing though. Boys are stupid.'

'He was young,' I said, 'but I should have known what kind of responses we'd get whatever the age. I have enough brothers to know what boys are really like and most of them never grow up mentally past the age of twelve. My brother Lewis is nineteen going on ten, and my half-brother Ethan is thirty going on . . . fifteen – he's more grown-up but not much. Dylan on the other hand is twelve going on fifty. He's a strange boy. Mum says he was born an old soul.'

'Same with my brothers,' said Zahrah. 'They are all little boys. Us girls run the house.'

'I can imagine,' I said. I'd only been to Zahrah's house once for a brief visit, but it was clear immediately on meeting her sisters and her mum that they wore the trousers.

Zahrah grinned. 'Women rule. Ah, here's another contender.' She approached a nice-looking boy who had stopped to look in a nearby window. She beckoned me to join her.

'Excuse us,' she said to the boy, who turned when she tapped him on the shoulder. 'We're doing a survey. Please could you tell us what your perfect girl would be like? As in soulmate?'

The boy grinned. He had a nice face, open and friendly. 'Hmm,' he said. 'There are lots of perfect girls around but, if you're talking soulmate, then I'd have to say she'd be a he because I'm gay.'

Hah. That shut Zahrah up.

'Perfect boy then,' I said, taking over.

The boy smiled. 'Oh the usual, someone you can talk to, have a laugh with and the chemistry has to be there. Someone who makes your knees buckle. Know what I mean?'

I nodded. *What a shame*, I thought as he walked on. *The only decent boy we meet out here and he's gay. Still lucky for some other gay boy somewhere.*

'Come on,' said Zahrah. 'Let's go and join Leela. See how she and Brook are getting on.'

We made our way across the road where Leela was questioning a couple of boys with Brook standing by and writing down the replies. The boys looked about sixteen, one with totally mad hair, long, spiky and sticking out in all directions, and the other with cropped dark hair.

'Good looks,' said the wild-haired boy. 'Very important. Enthusiasm and confidence. I like confident girls. And intelligent.'

'That's four things,' said Leela. 'I only asked you for three.'

'Oh and I like girls that smell nice, like of apple shampoo or something like that,' he added

Leela held up five fingers. 'That's five now.'

The boy looked at me. 'Your mate's bossy, isn't she?'

'Tell me about it,' I said and pointed at Zahrah. 'But she's nothing compared to Miss Scary Boots here. You should be glad she's not asking the questions.'

'So question two,' said Leela. 'What turns you off about girls?'

The boy moved a step closer to Leela. 'Wimpy girls who act like they couldn't even change a lightbulb. I like girls who are assertive —'

'I can't *stand* girls who are always on about being on a diet,' the dark-haired boy suddenly interrupted. 'And I hate girls who whinge or are loud or depressed or too demanding, like, Ooo, I'm a princess and you're my slave. And I don't like girls who are too clingy either, like, Why haven't you phoned me? When are we seeing each other again? Where've you been? Who with? Like, give me a *break*.'

We all burst out laughing. 'Oh poor baby,' said Zahrah. 'Sounds like you've known some demanding girls.'

'Yeah,' he said, then he turned to look at her properly and his eyes twinkled. 'I don't like difficult or demanding but . . . I definitely like a challenge.'

'Do you now?' asked Zahrah and she met his gaze and held it for a few moments. She had a twinkle in her eye too.

Brook and I exchanged glances. There was major flirtation going on in front of us. We decided to give Leela and Zahrah some space, so we linked arms and sauntered off to interview some boys of our own.

The rest of the afternoon was a great laugh and by the end

of our 'survey', Leela had two boys' phone numbers and Zahrah had a date with her boy called Ryan. Brook was asked for her number but she had decided to hold out for someone really special and told the boy who had asked her that she only dated scientists because she had a thing about Bunsen burners. He looked at her as though she was mad. We'd bumped into some boys from our school at one point, including Eddie O'Neil and we tried the survey on them. As he always did when he saw me, Eddie flirted like mad but, although his attention was flattering, I couldn't kid myself that I fancied him, even though he was tall, blond and athletic-looking. There was no one all afternoon who came even close to making my heart beat faster or having even a tiny bit of the effect on me that Joe did. But I didn't mind too much. I'd had a fun time and there would be other days – Leela's way of getting talking to boys was a good one and had given me hope.

After I'd left the girls, I set off down the main road then turned into a quieter street that led to home. In my mind, I started putting together the outfits that I might take to Italy at the end of the following week. After I'd sorted out a few, I got out my phone to call Erin to see if she had spoken to Scott as well as to fill her in on my hilarious day. She would have loved it, and she'd have been a star interviewer if she'd been here. I called her number and held the phone up to my ear. I could feel myself smiling even before she answered.

They came out of nowhere.

'Wu . . . arggghhh!!' I cried as someone grabbed me from

behind. I felt a hand clamp over my mouth and another cover my eyes, and I was pulled back off my feet by somebody behind me and, whoever he was, he stank of cigarette smoke.

A third hand grabbed my phone out of my hand and a male voice demanded. 'Give us your purse.'

'Hmmnuh,' I muttered through the palm over my mouth. I felt the grip loosen a little. I was terrified. I could hardly breath, never mind talk. My heart was beating like it had grown and was too big for my chest. I tried to twist away from the hands on my face but the person behind tightened their grip.

'Hurry up,' he said.

'I . . . I haven't got a purse. I . . .' I dug my hands into my jeans and pulled out the five pound note that I had left of my pocket money. 'Here. Take this. It's all I have.' We'd been told so many times in school that, if we were ever mugged, not to put up a fight but just to hand over what they wanted. I could hear Mrs Goldman's voice saying, 'You can always get another mobile phone or bit of cash, you can't get another life.' As I remembered her words, I felt even more panic. *What if one of them had a knife?*

'OI!' I heard a male voice cry in the distance. 'Leave her alone!' I tried to writhe around while at the same time cry out in response, but the hand over my mouth clamped tighter and, in doing so, he yanked my neck back.

'LET HER GO!' someone shouted and I could hear the sound of footsteps approaching.

'Leg it,' said one of my assailants. 'Someone's coming.'

The hands released me and I fell back on to the pavement with a thud. I turned my head to see the backs of two boys running down an alleyway to my right. Then they leapt over a wall and disappeared.

Seconds later, a third boy was towering over me. He looked about eighteen, tall, dark-skinned with brown eyes. He kneeled down, leaned over and offered his hand. I shrank back.

'It's OK,' he said. 'I won't hurt you. And I think I scared them off.' He took my hand and squeezed it gently. 'Are you OK?' He helped me into a sitting position and I rubbed the back of my head. I'd hit the pavement with quite a bang.

'I . . . I . . .'

'Can you stand up?' asked the boy.

I nodded and he helped me to my feet. Once up, I felt myself begin to shake. Once I'd started shaking, I couldn't stop. I couldn't control it and my backside hurt where I'd fallen. The boy looked up and down the street. 'Did they take much?' he asked.

'My phone and some money.'

'But you're OK?' he asked.

I nodded. Then I burst into tears.

Chapter 8

Mystery Boy

Getting home was a blur. I knew that the boy accompanied me, but everything seemed unreal, like I was in a dream. I felt very shaken, in shock that someone had penetrated the bubble I usually walk around in. School. Home. Fridge. Bed. Friends. Family. India Jane world. Safe and sound. Muggings happened to other people, not to me. I'd read about them in the newspaper but it always happened to someone else. Not this time. My world had changed, like anything could happen. However, I felt that the boy who helped me to my feet was a friend. His face was full of concern for me and the hand he offered was strong and kind. He told me that his name was Tyler and I must have given him my address because he knew where to bring me, and he must have rung the bell when we got to the house. It was weird, like I was disconnected from my brain.

Tyler kept reassuring me that I was all right. It was over. The boys had gone. As we walked home, I was so thankful that he was there. He felt like a solid presence, unphased by what had happened, in charge of getting me home and thankfully in no hurry to leave me to make my own way. As we walked, he told me about a course on journalism that he'd been on that afternoon and I was grateful for his chatter. It distracted me from going over what had happened in my head.

Mum answered the door and I vaguely remember her look of curiosity on seeing me with a strange boy changing to an expression of horror when Tyler told her that I had been mugged, and then she clasped me to her in a big hug. In typical Ruspoli style, soon the whole family knew and, shortly after I'd got back, I was sitting on one of the sofas in the front room between Dad and Dylan, who both had their arms around me, while Mum brought mugs of hot chocolate. It felt wonderful to be home, like Christmas had come early and it was touching to see how much each member of the family seemed to be affected by what had happened – even Kate came down to see if I was OK. It was only after Lewis had arrived that I stopped shaking and started to feel more like my normal self.

'So go over it again,' said Lewis, who had been told the whole story by Mum. 'Who was the boy who brought you back here?'

'Tyler,' I said.

'No surname?' asked Lewis.

Mum shook her head. 'Nice-looking boy. He had a good face and seemed responsible.'

'Where did he go?' I asked.

'That I don't know,' said Mum. 'I asked him in but he said he had to be somewhere. Once he knew that you were home safely, he wanted to be off.'

'I never said thank you,' I said. 'I'd like to ring him or send a card. He called out and the other boys ran off.'

'A veritable knight in shining Armani,' said Kate. 'A cutie. I saw him going down the path from my bedroom window.'

I hadn't really registered his fanciability at the time but, when I thought about him, I realised that he was, as Mum had said, a nice-looking boy – tall, slim with an intelligent, handsome face, but it was more than his looks – there was something grounded about him, like he knew where he was going and how to handle himself. *Bollards*, I thought. *All the boy hunting that we'd been doing all week with no luck and I meet a fabster who is kind, good-looking and a hero and I let him slip away. I hope I see him again.* Mum seemed to pick up on my thoughts.

'Maybe he'll call again,' she said.

'Hope so,' I said. 'He was almost like the perfect boy.'

'Pff. No such thing,' said Kate. 'If they're male, you have to compromise,'

'Sexist,' said Dad.

'Yeah, speak for yourself,' said Lewis. 'The girls I go out with don't have to compromise.'

'You think? And have you ever asked one of them?' asked Kate.

'Yeah, maybe you're not God's gift to women like you think you are,' said Dylan.

So much for being the centre of attention for long in this house, I thought as my family all dived in with their opinions about Lewis and his attitude to girls. I was about to join in but when I looked at Kate, I saw that she looked pale and her eyes were red.

'Has something happened?' I asked.

'Not really. Just a row with Tom.'

All eyes turned towards Kate.

'What happened?' asked Mum.

'When?' asked Dylan.

'Did you dump him?' asked Lewis.

'It was a quarrel, OK? No biggie,' said Kate, and I could see that she wished that she'd never mentioned anything.

'So does that mean it's over?' asked Dylan.

'*No,*' said Kate and she began to edge out of the room. 'Look. Forget it. Relationships are about good times and bad. You ride the storms.'

Dad gave Mum an affectionate look. 'Quite right,' he said.

'Compromise,' said Lewis smugly.

Kate hit him just before she left the room.

After more hugs and cuddles, it was time for me to go up to bed. Mum asked if I wanted her to tuck me in and read me a bedtime story like when I was five, but I was beginning to feel better and I wanted to talk to Erin about what had happened and then have some time on my own to go over the events of the day and let it sink in that, yes, it had been horrible but it was over. It *was* over. And I was home and safe. As I went upstairs, I thought about what Kate had said. 'Relationships are about good times and bad.' *Did that mean that there might be hope for Joe and me after all? I wondered. All I had to do was weather the storm.* 'Compromise,' Lewis's voice rang in my head. *Boy, this love thing is complicated,* I thought.

My black and white kittens, Posh and Becks, were cuddled up together at the end of my bed and both looked up, hoping to be made a fuss of, as I sat at my desk and picked up the phone. When they saw that I wasn't going to get on the bed with them, Posh put her head down and went back to sleep, but Becks got up and came and sat on my lap then tried to climb on to my shoulder and nuzzle my nose. He was such a sweetie. I stroked him for a while then dialled Erin's number. Her mum picked up and called her to come to the phone.

'Hey India. How goes it?' she said a few minutes later.

'My turn to need to hear your voice this time,' I said.

'Why? What's happened?'

'I got mugged today.'

'You WHADDDTTTTTTTT? When? Where? Are you OK?'

I quickly filled her in on all the details.

'Jeez. Sure you're OK?'

'Yeah. Fine now.'

'I wish I was there and I could give you a big hug.'

'Me too. But I'm OK, don't worry. They got my phone and some cash, but I'm fine.

'Sure?' asked Erin.

'Double sure,' I said. 'Do you think we should go on to MSN – this call will be costing a fortune. I just wanted to hear your voice for a few minutes.'

'Nah. There are times when it is absolutely permissible to run up our parents' phone bills and this is one of them. Stay on the phone. Will you see this Tyler again?'

'I hope so. He had a good vibe. He made me feel safe.'

'Could it be love?'

I laughed. It felt good to be talking boys instead of muggings. 'Duh. What is love? I don't know.'

'Me neither. I've been thinking about it lately. I mean, it's such a general word. Like we say, I love my mum; I love chocolate. Totally different levels.'

'Yeah. I love my cats too. And I love my friends but that's a different kind of love too, isn't it?'

'And what you feel for a boy is different again. Like what you felt for Joe.'

'Yeah but that kind of love can do your head in. Love for family and friends is the best; they're really there for you when you need them.'

'Yeah. Boys come and go but friends are for ever. Have you let Leela, Brook and Zahrah know?'

'Not yet. I . . . I wanted to talk to you first.'

'Quite right. Bezzies first – but they'll want to know.'

'I'll tell them at school when they're all there. To be honest it all felt a bit unreal earlier on. After my family, I didn't think of talking to anyone except you.'

'Sure you're OK, India?'

'Yeah. Honest. But what about you? I was about to call and ask how things were with Scott when my phone got swiped. Any news?'

'No. I called his mobile again but it's still switched off. I did call his landline though and his mum picked up. She said that he'd gone into town this afternoon, so it sounds as if at least he got home last night or she'd have said something. I'll see how it goes. Maybe I'll see him around school, but I need to get him alone; it's not a conversation I want to have while his mates are around.'

'Yeah. Very wise. Plus we all know how boys can act differently when there's a gang of them.'

'Specially Scott. Like he's always got to act the big man.'

'Let me know how it goes, OK?'

'I will. And hey, aren't you off to Italy soon?'

'End of next week. Can't wait.'

'Just what you need after a shake-up, India. Sure you're OK now?'

'Yep. Bit tired now.'

'Me too. Off to bed then. Sweet dreams, lady of the red, white and blue land.'

'Sweet dreams, lady of the green land. Love ya.'

'Love you too.'

Chapter 9

Italy

Zahrah, Brook and Leela were so sweet when they heard about what had happened and all week they treated me like a princess, bringing me choccie treats and magazines to cheer me up and even helping me set up the address book on my new mobile. The story of my mugging spread around the school like a flu virus and by Friday lunchtime, because of a lack of any other news that week, I was a celebrity. Everywhere I went, people turned and stared or did a double take then whispered to their friends.

'Hey India, did you know that you had your head kicked in and are now in hospital with brain damage and a broken leg? The rumour is that you may never walk again,' said Leela as she came out of the school canteen at lunchtime. 'I just heard Ruby and Nicole in the lunch queue.'

Zahrah raised her eyebrows. 'Typical,' said Zahrah. (Ruby and Nicole were two girls who I almost got in with in the first half of term, but then I realised that they liked to gossip about people all the time and a lot of it was really unkind or exaggerated to make a big drama.)

I nodded. 'No wonder some people are staring. People must think I've made a rapid recovery. I overheard some other girls talking in the girls' cloakroom and, apparently, my hero Tyler is a black belt in karate and he kung fu-ed and karate-chopped my muggers into oblivion.'

We linked arms and made our way to our favourite radiator outside the sports hall. 'And I heard that there were six muggers and Tyler floored them all,' said Zahrah.

'Maybe you should release a statement for the school magazine,' said Brook. 'India Jane is alive and well and hasn't missed a day of school.'

'I could,' I said, 'but it's good to have a bit of fun after what happened. I like hearing just how far the Chinese whispers will go. I just wish Tyler would get in touch so I could thank him properly.'

'With a big snog,' said Brook.

'Still no word from him?' asked Leela.

'Disappeared into thin air.'

When we got to our radiator, there were three girls from Year Nine lounging there.

Zahrah gave them a look as if to say, 'That's our place.'

They took no notice and a small blonde one nudged her

friends when she saw me. 'Hey. Aren't you India Jane Ruspoli?'

I nodded.

'Aren't you supposed to be in a coma?' she asked.

'She is,' said Zahrah. 'She's a zombie. The undead walking the corridors of school. I'd get out of her way now if I were you, before she rips off your arm and hits you with the soggy end.'

'Take no notice of her,' I said. 'I was in a coma but my friends came in and sang songs from *The Sound of Music* to me and that brought me back.'

Zahrah, Brook and Leela nodded. 'It was like a miracle,' said Leela in a trembly voice that sounded as if she was near to tears. 'We thought we'd lost her.'

Brook burst into the song that the nuns sing in the movie. '*Climb every mountain,*' she warbled in a silly voice.

'*Ford every stream,*' Zahrah and Leela joined in while I put my hand on my heart, nodded and looked gratefully at them.

The Year Nine girls' eyes grew large and then the tallest of them screwed up her nose. 'Pff. They're winding us up,' she said to her mates. 'Come on, let's go.'

They slunk off down the corridor, leaving us to lean up against the radiator and get toasty warm.

'We really ought to have a system in place for the future though,' said Zahrah, 'so that we can see each other safely home.'

'Seems mad to have to do that in broad daylight,' I said. 'I think the best thing is that, if we have to go home alone, we stick to the busier streets. I should have known better than to go down the road I did – it's always quiet and there are a couple of alleyways there where people can hide.'

'My mum makes me and Ranjiv carry two mobile phones since he got mugged last year,' said Leela. 'An old one that doesn't work and isn't worth anything in our pocket so that if anyone grabs us and demands our phones, we can hand them over. And she says to keep the good ones in our rucksacks.'

'Good idea,' I said. 'I should do that and tell Dylan to as well.'

'Yeah but I keep forgetting,' said Leela, 'and I carry both of them in my pocket. I won't in future though. Talking of which, are you looking forward to Italy?'

I nodded. We were going later that day. I'd packed my bag the previous night, and Dad was going to be waiting outside school at the end of the afternoon with our cases to whisk us away to the airport. I couldn't wait.

'Will there be any boys at your grandmother's party?' asked Brook.

'Maybe,' I replied. 'A few.'

'Anyone you know or fancy?' asked Leela.

I shook my head. 'Not unless there's someone new there – it's mainly going to be family and I know most of my cousins.'

Brook looked disappointed. 'No one?' she asked. 'There must be *one* boy over there.'

'There's Bruno. His parents own the hotel we're staying at.'

'Why are you staying in a hotel?' asked Zahrah. 'I thought you had loads of family over there.'

'We do but Nonna's house is packed out already. It's going to be a big do. Loads of people will be staying at the hotel. Dad's known the owners since he was a boy and I used to play there when I was little.'

'Weeth Bruno,' said Leela in an Italian accent.

I nodded.

'Rewind a mo,' said Brook. 'So who's Nonna?'

'Nonna is Italian for grandmother,' I explained.

'Tell us more about Bruno,' said Leela. 'I like his name.'

'You *so* wouldn't be interested in him. He put a frog in my bed once and thought it was really funny. My main memory is of trying to get away from him because, when he wasn't finding insects or creatures to annoy me with, he wanted to fight. I won once and he got really sulky and said that hair pulling, which was my technique, was girl fighting. But Bruno as potential boyfriend material? Never in a million years. He was a clumsy oaf with a face like a potato which, no doubt, he still has. He isn't my type at all.'

Leela laughed. 'Sounds like love to me,' she said.

'When did you last see him?' asked Zahrah.

'Ages ago. He was twelve and I was nine.'

'Haven't you been over there since then?' asked Brook.

'Yeah, we go every year to see Nonna, but he's been away when we've visited the last few times – at summer camps and on school trips, stuff like that.'

'So he's three years older than you,' said Zahrah. 'He'll be eighteen or nineteen now and might have grown up to be a babe.'

I laughed. 'Bruno? Hah. I think you can pretty well see how boys are going to turn out, so – fanciable? *No* way but hopefully there will be some other boys there. You never know.'

The afternoon flew by and, by four o'clock, Kate, Dylan and I were squashed in the back of the car and Mum and Dad were in the front. Lewis was meeting us at the airport and Aunt Sarah, Ethan and his wife Jessica and their twins had gone out on a morning flight. Kate and I did a good cruise of the airport shops once we got to Heathrow and I bought a magazine for the journey and some lip-gloss at duty free. On board the plane, I fell asleep for what felt like a few minutes and then we were landing at Naples airport.

'Hope the brakes work,' said Dylan when we touched down with a soft thud and the noise from the plane engine grew into an earsplitting roar as we careered down the runway.

After getting off the plane and collecting our luggage, we made our way out to the car park where the black Mercedes that Nonna had sent for us was waiting. Once in the car, we settled back into the leather seats, and Kate and I listened to our iPods for a while, then Dylan and I played word games to pass the time because it was dark outside and we couldn't see anything out of the window. Usually this is my favourite car ride in the world – the Amalfi coastline is stunning. On this particular night, all we could see were the lights of Naples in the distance, more lights as we drove past Sorrento, Positano and Amalfi and fewer as we got on to a mountain road which wound around and around up to Ravello.

'Here at last,' said Dad after an hour and a half and we saw a dimly lit narrow cobbled street in the near distance.

Our driver drove into the street through an ancient-looking archway then parked the car and we all got out and stretched our legs. I breathed in the air. It smelled different immediately, fresh and fragrant with a scent I couldn't place – something herby and sharp. A middle-aged man appeared from nowhere and he and the driver unloaded our baggage on to an open trolley like the ones you find at the airport, only this one had a driver's seat at the back, like on a tractor. After the cases were all piled up, the man began to drive along the street in the direction of our hotel. Everything for that end of town goes up on these trolleys because the streets are too narrow for cars, and it is a regular sight to see trolleys loaded down with boxes of supplies going past.

Dad was beaming from ear to ear. 'OK, everybody follow me. Dinner in the square before we go up to the hotel.' He put his arm around Mum and off they marched.

Kate, Dylan, Lewis and I followed him into the square where we soon saw people we knew sitting at one of the open cafés that surrounded the cobbled piazza. It was a warm night and felt more like summer than November. Dad was in his element going from table to table hugging and smiling as he greeted old friends. It seemed like the whole Ruspoli family had gathered there: aunts, uncles, cousins, Ethan, Jessica and the twins – and Nonna, who seemed overjoyed to see all her family. She's a tall handsome woman with silver-grey hair pulled back into an elegant bun. She wrapped me in her arms when she saw me.

'India Jane, look how tall you have become since last time. And beautiful, *bella*,' she said with a smile.

I hugged her back and then, as others came forward to greet her, I moved away so that they could have their turn. It was then that I spotted a boy at a corner table and my heart stopped. He was a total babe, so good-looking he had to be a model. Tall with a mane of dark hair and a chiselled jaw, he was wearing a tweedy overcoat with a red scarf and jeans and exuded glamour and elegance. He glanced over when Dad called for me to sit at the table next to his and then he did a double take.

'India Jane! *Chi e? E tu?*' he asked.

I felt myself blush as I tried to muster up my Italian. 'Do I know you? Er . . . *Si . . . Lo . . . Ti conosce?* Is that right? Do I know you? Er . . . *Mi dispiace ma non parlo Italiano bene. Infatto e robaccia.* Ohmigod! Bruno!'

Chapter 10

Lunch in Ravello

Send photos! demanded Erin, Brook, Leela and Zahrah after I'd texted to let them know that Bruno had grown up to be a love god.

We had spent a fab night having supper in the square and, because there were so many people to see and catch up with, I only got to talk to Bruno for a few minutes. However, every time I glanced over at where he was sitting, he looked up and caught me watching him. Or he'd been glancing over and I'd turn and catch him. It happened so many times that it was impossible to pretend that we weren't totally checking each other out. In the end, we both laughed and when the meal was finished, coffees and limoncellos had been drunk by the adults and people were beginning to wander off in the direction of their hotels, he came over to me and gave me a warm hug.

'*Non fa niente. C'incontriamo e parliamo domani. D'accordo?*' he asked, which I quickly translated in my head to mean: Let's get together and catch up properly tomorrow, shall we?

'*Si, d'accordo,*' I replied which I hope meant OK. 'Um . . . as long as there are no . . . oh what's the word for . . .' I made a noise like a frog. 'A . . . you know, frog?'

'Frog. In Italian is *rana.*'

'Oh yes.'

'Is OK, speak English with me. It is good for me to practise,' he said.

'And my dad would say it's good for me to practise my Italian but I doubt you'd understand much.'

'Then speak English. I won't tell him. So you were saying? Frogs?'

I nodded. 'Yes, I'd love to catch up as long as there are no frogs and no fighting. Er let me see if I can say that . . . *Si, d'accordo. Ma senza rane e senza pugnati.*'

He laughed. 'Very good. Ah *si*, I remember – I used to put them into your bed.' Then he looked directly into my eyes and I felt my insides melt. 'No frogs,' he said. 'I promise.' His expression grew cheeky. 'Unless . . . there's one that needs kissing to turn him back into a prince.'

I looked around the square as if I was searching for someone. 'Can't see any frogs,' I said.

'Shame,' he said, then he made a frog noise which made me crack up laughing. 'OK. Night, India. *Ciao, bella.*'

'*Ciao,*' I said, and I inwardly punched the air as he walked away and disappeared up one of the narrow streets that led away from the square.

Kate came over and looked after him. 'Well, get you,' she said.

'What do you mean?' I asked and tried to sound innocent, but I knew that I had a great big smile on my face.

'Bruno, huh?'

'We were just chatting. Er . . . What's he up to now?' I asked because I'd seen her talking to him over supper.

'Student,' she replied. 'Doing business studies. He wants to go into hotel management, follow in the family business. He's going to be a very rich boy one day – his dad owns three hotels in the area now.'

'Three? Wow. Er . . . Do you fancy him?'

Kate looked in the direction Bruno had gone off in. 'Who wouldn't? But chill, it looks like he only has eyes for you so you're safe. Besides Tom would kill me.'

Phew, I thought. I'd hate to compete with Kate. She wasn't just stunning to look at, she could also out cool anyone and most boys seemed to love that. Luckily her relationship with Tom seemed back on track.

Our hotel was behind a tall wall on the hill beyond the main square. I woke the next morning, scrambled out of bed and flung open the shutters to a picture-postcard view of brilliant blues and greens – fields on the mountain opposite were terraced all the way down into the valley, sea in the distance where boats looked like toys, the jagged coastline jutting out and stretching on into the distance.

'India,' groaned Kate as she pulled a sheet over her head. 'Close the shutters.'

'Oh come on, Kate, it's a beautiful morning. We're in Ravello —'

'And India has the hots for a local boy so has to wake up the world,' said Kate, looking at her watch. 'It's eight-thirty. Go and get me a coffee and maybe I'll forgive you.'

I pulled on my jeans and a red jumper and happily set off to get breakfast. *I feel on top of the world*, I said to myself as I hopped down the stairs, *which is funny because I almost am.* The hotel hadn't changed since my childhood. The interior was dark and cool in contrast to the sun sneaking in through the open windows and casting its light on heavy walnut furniture and marble floors. I had always liked the fact that the hotel had the look of a private house with antique-looking books stacked here and there and sepia photos of unsmiling people looking out from silver frames. I often wondered who they were – they looked like farmers from a long gone era, dressed in their best black with stiff collars for the photo. As I passed through the hall, I noticed a huge bowl full of oranges and their scent which filled the air.

I could see that some of the family were already down so I sneaked into the dining room, poured a cup of coffee from the tall dresser on the side and took it up to Kate, who had dozed off again. Sleeping is one of Kate's talents, along with posing and looking cool.

Back downstairs, the atmosphere was like a wedding with people talking about what they were going to wear for the lunch party and how the day was going to unfold. All I knew was that I was looking forward to seeing Bruno again and wanted to pick my outfit very carefully. I put several outfits together in my head from what I'd brought while I tucked into freshly baked pastries, drank a perfect cappuccino and gazed out of the window at the view. Just as I was finishing, I saw through the open door that Bruno had arrived and was talking to the man behind the desk in the reception area at the front of the hall. He waved when he saw me and came over. He looked pleased to see me.

'India,' he said. '*Ciao.* I was hoping to catch you. Have you got plans for the day yet?'

'I . . .'

Dad got up from the table nearby and came over and slapped Bruno on the back.

'Bruno. *Allora. E dando caccia a mia figlia? E vero?*'

He'd asked, are you after my daughter then? I wanted to die – whatever cool I had managed to muster melted like an ice lolly in the sun. 'Da-*ad.*'

Bruno laughed. He didn't seemed phased by Dad's bluntness. '*Si. E perche no! Non e difficile capire perche.*'

I struggled to translate what he'd said. I think it was good and that he'd said, And why not? It's not hard to see why.

'Dad. Bruno. *Inglese per favore.* English please.'

'I said . . . She is beautiful, Mr Ruspoli. I want to whisk her

87

away for the morning, if that's OK with you.'

I felt myself blushing but I felt chuffed. I liked the fact that he was so straight-forward, so different to most English boys I knew who would never admit to fancying someone. It was refreshing to meet someone who was upfront about it.

'That OK with you, India?' Dad asked in his usual loud voice, and everyone in the restaurant stopped eating breakfast and watched us as if we were characters in a play.

'Um . . . yeah.'

'In Italian,' Dad demanded.

'*Si.*'

People went back to their breakfasts, apparently satisfied with my reply. Bruno tugged on my arm. 'Let's go then.'

I quickly ran upstairs to grab my camera phone, then off we went. As I followed him down the lane and around the town, I felt as if I was walking through a romantic movie set. Bruno took me to Villa Ruffola, an old monastery down the steps from our hotel and just off the square through an ancient-looking wooden gate. It had lovely gardens with sculpted trees in enormous pots and benches hidden amongst the shrubbery from where you could sit and stare at the stunning views across the valley. Here and there was a white statue of a naked god or goddess and I couldn't help but notice how they all had perfect bums. *Must have been all that hill climbing,* I thought. *Good for the buttocks.*

Bruno produced a camera.

'Stand by the statue,' he said.

I did as I was told and then stood in the same position as the statue, with my hand on my hip and my chin raised.

Bruno clicked the camaera. '*Bella,*' he said. 'You are beautiful.'

After the gardens, we went back to the square and sat outside the restaurant where we had eaten the night before. We had cappuccinos and watched tourists climbing the steps of the cathedral, went into a couple of pottery shops, bought postcards, took photos. After that we walked, we talked and he took me into one of the five star hotels on the other side of the square to where my family was staying, partly to see the spectacular view from up there but also I think to show off – all the staff seemed to know him and greeted him in a friendly and respectful manner. One of the waiters offered to take a picture of us and I made a note to send it to my mates.

I found out a lot about Bruno as the hours slipped by. He was a Gemini, like me. He'd had a girlfriend until last year and they had split up because he felt it wasn't going anywhere. He liked travelling, he liked world music – his favourite being anything with an Arabic sound, he liked art and talked about the post-modern period, which I had to admit I didn't know a lot about but I made a note to look up when I got back to England. I loved being in his company and kept sneaking glances at him when I thought he wasn't looking. He was like a work of art himself and I felt on a high to be with him. In turn, he kept looking at me and smiling.

'You ask many questions, India Jane.'

'Sorry,' I said. 'I tend to do that. I'm interested in people.'

'Don't be sorry. I like it. I like that you want to know all about me. And now I want to ask about you because don't forget that I am Gemini too.' And so he fired all my questions back at me and it was only when he asked if I had a boyfriend that I realised that I hadn't thought about Joe once since I had met Bruno – and that was a record because, most days, I thought about Joe every hour.

'Not exactly,' I replied. I didn't want to admit that the one boy I was in love with didn't want to know. 'I . . . It's complicated. I'm sort of between boys. It didn't work out with one,' (I thought that a half-truth would do) 'and . . . er . . . I've just met someone new.'

'Me too!' Bruno beamed. Actually I had meant Tyler, and I had been about to tell the half-truth about him in order to make it sound like I had a whole coachload of boys after me. Erin used to tell me that boys often want what other boys want. It's an ego thing with them, and the more desired by others that you appear to be, then the more they desire you.

'Might be you,' I said with a smile. 'Might not.'

'In that case . . .' said Bruno, and as he took my hand, I felt a frisson of electricity run through me, '. . . I am going to have to win you over.' He looked directly into my eyes and my stomach lurched like he was pulling me towards him.

'Like a knight of old,' I said. *If only he knew the truth*, I thought. I was his from the second I saw him.

When it got closer to Nonna's lunch, we walked hand in hand back to the hotel and for a few minutes we stood outside the arch that led to the gardens. He leaned towards me and hesitated. I looked at his lovely face and leaned towards him, then leaned back. We met each other's eyes and laughed. We knew that we were both thinking the same thing. Our first kiss. When should it be?

He took a breath as if getting back control, kissed me lightly on the forehead and gently pushed me towards the gardens. 'Later, *amore*,' he said.

I nodded, turned and ran to get dressed.

Every moment away from him was too long, like I had been eating a bowl of the most divine ice cream and it had been wrenched away from me.

I texted the girls in London and Erin in Ireland and sent off the photo. *M in lurrrrve. Have fnd prfct boy*, I wrote.

Erin was first to respond. *Ohmigod. He is gorgissimo. I am in lurve too. Has he got a twin?*

My outfit for the lunch was a dress of rust-coloured silk that Mum had picked out for me. It had a halter-neck and flared out from my waist in a swirl to my knees. Aunt Sarah had lent me her aubergine cashmere pashmina and some amber drop-earrings to wear with it. I went downstairs to find Mum and Dad and they beamed when they saw me.

'India,' Mum said. 'You look a picture.'

'Those colours are perfect on you,' said Dad. 'My little girl all grown-up.'

I couldn't help grinning. I felt grown-up, sophisticated. I was in one of the most beautiful places in the world with my family and I thought I was falling in love with a boy who liked me too. Life couldn't be better.

Everyone had dressed up for the lunch. Mum looked stunning in an off-the-shoulder sea-green dress which made her eyes look greener than ever. Aunt Sarah was wearing a chic black linen dress with a big shell necklace that suited her dark hair and brown eyes. All the boys were wearing suits, even Dylan, who looked so cute, and for once Kate, who normally lived in jeans, had made an effort and was wearing a red silk dress with her hair loose down her back. With her customary big black sunglasses, she looked like an A-list celebrity. Outside the weather was still unseasonably warm as the family made their way en masse up the lane to the villa where lunch was being held. After winding our way up the slopes and several sets of steps, we turned into an old wooden doorway where a path was lined with urns full of pink and red geraniums still in bloom. At the top of the path was Nonna's house – a tall white villa with green shutters and a wrought iron veranda. I'd loved going there and had always fantasised that, one day, I would have a home just like hers with cool interiors, beautiful gardens and a view to die for. In her garden were monkey puzzle trees and Cyprus trees to the left, a statue of four cherubs to the right and, behind them, the mountains and the sea. One of the cherubs was missing an arm. I smiled as I remembered why. When we were little, Lewis had run for a ball, tripped and reached out for one of the cherubs. As he fell, he took its arm with him. Nonna had never told him off for running as Dad did later when he heard about the incident, but gave him ice cream instead.

We made our way inside where other family members had already gathered in the hall. The decor was of the same period as the hotel, with panelled walls and dark wood antique furniture, and everyone was chatting and laughing while waiters dressed in black and white handed out bellinis and canapés. I inhaled deeply. The smell of beeswax polish and lavender took me right back to when I was tiny and first visited Nonna here.

'A drink for the Cinnamon Girl,' said Dad. He handed me a flute of the champagne and peach juice, and waiters began to usher us through to the back of the villa to a room which was set for lunch. It looked lovely, as if set for a wedding and, for a nanosecond, I imagined it was mine and Bruno's. Each table had a white cloth and a centrepiece of gold winter pansies. In the middle of the room, Nonna sat looking every inch the matriarch of the family. Like Aunt Sarah, she was wearing black linen and she looked so stylish and happy as she greeted all her family.

I took my present (a framed painting I had done of Nonna's villa) and put it on a table near the doorway with the others. I was about to turn away when Bruno came up and stood behind me. I leaned back against him and he nuzzled into my neck. I really wanted to turn around, but I thought that our first kiss should definitely not be in full view of my relatives. He smelled divine, of lemon and Cyprus (I know which scents are which because of Mum making her bath oils and perfumes for Aunt Sarah's shop). His scent made my stomach contract in a way that felt lovely. He caught my hand and we walked into the room. Lewis raised an eyebrow and grinned and I smiled back. I didn't even mind if he or Dad said something uncool – nothing could ruin this day. Bruno went to sit with his family while I went to sit with mine, but we kept glancing at each other all through the lunch. It was like he was a magnet and I couldn't take my eyes off him and he clearly felt the same – like we had a secret that no one else was in on.

At first I could hardly eat. I struggled through the first course of Parma ham and, by the time the main course of pasta arrived, I had no appetite. But, when the waiters brought chocolate mousse and raspberries, it was so delicious that I had to have mine *and* the half of Mum's that she couldn't finish. *Chocolate mousse is the food of love*, I told myself as I licked my spoon.

After everyone had eaten, there were several speeches and Dad's in particular got a lot of laughs as he recalled the time when he was a boy and drove his mother insane with his singing and rehearsing the piano and whatever other instrument he could lay his hands on. Nonna listened to it all with a smile and tears in her eyes. After the speeches, various family members got up and did their party piece. Dad and his brother Fabio sang a wonderful duet. Dylan played the piano. One of my cousins who is nine danced some ballet. An old auntie recited a piece of poetry. Her husband sang some opera. The atmosphere was wonderful. A truly happy occasion.

As the tables were cleared away, some of the adults moved outside to enjoy the view, while inside a space was made for a dance floor. Bruno came to join me as soon as the disco music began to play, putting his arms around me and holding me close. We danced a little and made up our own steps for a few numbers, and then the DJ played a ballad and Bruno pulled me even closer. *I am in heaven*, I thought as I closed my eyes and let my head lean against his shoulder. This feels so completely right. *We fit together.*

Suddenly Bruno took my hand and led me away from the dance floor.

'Where are we going?' I asked.

'You'll see,' he replied and he pulled my hand so that we were running. We went out of the villa, out of the grounds and further up the lane.

'I've been saving this for last,' he said. 'The best view in the whole of Ravello.'

We reached a wooden door similar to the one that led to Nonna's house and then walked past a lovely old house, through gardens, under a pergola and then out to a terrace where there were four pillars covered with an arched roof. Bruno put his hands over my eyes. 'Trust me,' he said as he pushed me gently forward.

We walked a few more steps and then he removed his hands. 'Now open your eyes.'

I did as I was told and there before me was the most stunning view of all. Mountains, coastlines and, far, far below the sea. I felt like I was standing up in the heavens gazing down – in fact, we were so high up, it made me feel dizzy. I stepped back to catch my breath and Bruno caught me, pulled me to him and looked deep into my eyes. I moved towards him then, at last, he pressed his lips on mine. The whole world disappeared around us and I returned his kiss with all the emotion that I could muster.

When we finally drew apart, we looked at each other and smiled. 'India Jane,' he said.

'Bruno,' I replied.

There was nothing else to be said.

Later that night, I sent a text to the girls. *M in luv.*

Chapter 11

Homeward Bound

Dad glanced at me in the car mirror. "'Time is too slow for those who wait, too swift for those who fear, too long for those who grieve, too short for those who rejoice, but for those who love, time is eternity'," he said as he drove us back through the streets of London. 'One of my favourite quotes by Henry Van Dyke.'

Mum turned around from the front seat of the car and gave my knee a squeeze. 'I have a quote about time too. It passes. And you'll be seeing him again before you know it.'

I was slumped in the back. Her words were no consolation. Nobody could *possibly* know how I felt about having to leave Bruno and not knowing when I'd see him again. I felt sore inside and out – a bit of lipsalve might have soothed the snog rash I had on my chin from our long kissing sessions. He was a great kisser and I had a few more pointers for Mikey when the time came for his snog lesson.

'I'll be over in England soon,' he'd said before we left as he held me to him. 'I have to come on hotel business. Don't be sad, *bella*. Neither time nor distance will keep us apart.'

But I knew that his visit might be weeks away, months even, and for each minute away from him I would be like a flower without the sun. A plant without water. I would grow thinner and paler and sadder. And droop. Like a droopy thing that's come over all poetic. Bruno had had a strange effect on me and all the love clichés that anyone had ever written or sung seemed like they now applied to me. We'd only had two days but I felt that it was true love. I had never felt like this about anyone who reciprocated before, and it seemed cruel that the one boy who I was clearly meant to be with lived in another country. We had spent every minute together that we could while in Ravello: after Nonna's lunch, late into the night (until Dad came to get me and marched me back to the hotel), and the next day up until the flight left. But the time had gone by too fast, and all too soon I was back in grey, cold dark England, alone. Droopy. In pain.

Dylan pinched my arm. 'So lover boy's in Italy,' he said. 'Get over it.'

I crossed my arms over my chest. 'Thanks for the sympathy.'

Dylan tapped the side of his nose and grinned. 'Before we left, he asked me to give you something when we got back to London.'

'So where is it?'

'You have to cheer up first,' said Dylan.

I did a fake smile, grabbed his arm and gave him a Chinese burn.

'Mu-*um*,' he whinged.

'Now you two, don't start,' said Mum. 'Dylan. Hand it over right now. It's not the time.'

I let go of his arm and he stuck his tongue out at me, but he did as Mum had told him and, scrabbling about in his rucksack, he pulled out a letter. I was going to stuff it in my bag to read in privacy when I got home, but I knew I couldn't wait. Luckily I had a tiny torch on the keyring that Lewis had given me last Christmas so I got that out, clicked it on and could just about make out what was there. It was a poem underneath which he had written a note. His handwriting was beautiful.

"When love beckons to you, follow him,
  Though his ways are hard and steep.
  And when his wings enfold you, yield to him,
  Though the sword hidden among his pinions may wound you.
  And when he speaks to you, believe in him,
  Though his voice may shatter your dreams as the north wind lays waste the garden."

India Jane, you have beckoned me and having to part from you is the hidden sword that I must endure. My only comfort is that I know that love has spoken to me. I believe in him and that we will be together again.

  Yours, Bruno XX

PS: The poem is a verse from a book called The Prophet *written by Kahlil Gibran.*

My eyes filled with tears. I didn't quite get what he was trying to say but it was lovely all the same. It was the most romantic thing that anyone had ever done for me. I held the paper to my heart and then to my nose and, as I had hoped, I caught a faint whiff of his scent on the paper. It smelled of citrus and wood and Italy. I stared out into the dark night and felt alone and yet at the same time at one with the thousands of lovers all over the world who were parted.

As soon as I got home, I sent my photos from Ravello over to Erin in Ireland and then I called her. I was so excited and sad and happy all at the same time that I needed to share it with her. It was only when I'd blabbed on about everything that had happened without drawing breath that I realised that Erin sounded subdued.

'Hey, are you OK?' I asked.

'Yeah. Least . . . yeah I am . . . Oh India, I don't know what to do. I'm glad you've had a fab weekend, I really am and I don't want to bring you down but . . .' She burst into tears.

'Hey, *hey*, Erin, what is it? Is it Scott again? Oh God, I am so sorry. I was all me me me when you're upset. What's happened?'

Erin sobbed a little longer and I didn't say much until the sobs subsided. Then she said, 'I'm . . . *sob* . . . sorry . . . I . . . didn't want to ruin your weekend . . .'

'Erin, you are my best mate in the world and nothing could ruin my weekend. Now, tell me what's happened.'

'It is Scott again. We were at a party on Saturday and he got completely out of it again. I found him curled up in a ball outside the back door. It was freezing out there and it took me ages to bring him round. I struggled to drag him inside. You know I've seen him drink and smoke before, but it's like he's going for oblivion. I just don't get it. He can't enjoy himself because he spends most of the nights out of it at parties these days, dead to the world. I tried to talk to him when he came round a bit and it couldn't have gone worse. He got so angry with me, called me awful names like he hated me, and then he stormed off with a spliff and a bottle of vodka. A full bottle. And that would be on top of what he'd already had. I am so worried that something awful is going to happen to him.'

'You *have* to tell someone, Erin. You can't deal with this on your own.'

'But who? I'm telling you. And I told you, it's not just the drink, it's what he's smoking too.'

'What about telling his mum?'

'No way. His mum is scary. Remember, she's a school governor? I can't imagine what she'd do.'

'Oh God, yeah, I remember her. Tall and skinny, yeah? Can't he talk to his dad? I know they're divorced but he's still sees Scott, doesn't he?'

'Not much. He moved to Australia not long after you moved to London.'

'Bummer. I didn't know that. Is there anybody at school?'

'He'd never forgive me. Oh God. I'm so sorry to lay all this on you when you've just got back but it's doing my head in.'

'Hey. It's me here. Mates, yeah? Listen. Let me think about it. What did your mates over there say after the party?'

'Stay away from him, stay out of it, but he is . . . or rather *was*, a mate too. I can't stand by and let him go under. Like remember when my mum was ill?'

'Yeah.'

'Well he was there for me as well as you. You both got me through it. I know he's got a good heart because I've seen it.'

'Let me talk to the girls over here,' I said. 'We'll think of something. Listen, get a good night's sleep. We'll sort it.'

'Thanks, India. And thanks for being my friend. And . . . Bruno looks divine. I'm really happy for you. Honest I am.'

'Me too,' I said. After we'd hung up, I looked at my photos of Bruno again. *Were you for real?* I wondered, going through the different shots. After listening to Erin talk, the weekend in Italy seemed like a lovely dream that I'd had and was already slipping away as reality took over. I read the poem that he'd sent again. *I'm not going to let this fade*, I thought as I tucked it into my pillow then got ready for school the next day.

Chapter 12

Love Hurts

'I'd try and talk to him when he was sober,' said Zahrah after I'd told them all about Erin's dilemma when we had our Monday morning catch-up at school. 'Absolutely no point in trying to argue with someone when they're out of their head. I remember once trying to talk to my second cousin at a wedding when he was drunk and he told me to get lost, get a life and some other very rude things, then he threw up all over my jacket. He was really apologetic the next day, but I don't think he remembered half of what he'd said or done. I hate boys when they're drunk out of their minds.'

'And girls,' said Brook. 'Remember that party we went to last Christmas and there were all those Sixth-Formers knocking back the Bacardi breezers like they were lemonade. It was sick city by one o'clock. The bathroom stee-ank.'

'And the kitchen. One of them threw up in the sink,' said Leela.

'Ergh! Gross,' said Brook.

'My mum says lesson numero uno when it comes to alcohol is don't mix your drinks,' I said. 'That way, you don't get sick.'

'Unless you drink too much,' said Brook.

'I'd get him a brochure from somewhere like Alcoholics Anonymous and send it to him anonymously,' said Leela. 'Sounds like he needs help and, if it comes from an outside place like AA, it may be easier for him to take than it coming from an old mate or from someone close. Boys are very proud and don't like being told what to do. Ranjiv would never take my advice about anything, not even about how he wears his hair.'

'I don't think Erin thinks that Scott's an alcoholic,' I said, 'least not yet. Just he drinks to excess and, when he smokes skunk, he turns nasty.'

'Hey. Remember that counsellor guy who came in to talk to us in PSHE last year about drink and drugs?' said Brook. 'He was brill. There's bound to be someone over there who does that sort of thing. I'd tell Erin to find someone like that and go to have a chat with him.'

'Plus, he ought to get real. He could really cop it if anyone finds him with drugs,' said Zahrah.

'I know but, to tell the truth, yes I care what happens to Scott but I'm more worried about Erin. She's really down about this. She's known him for years.'

Zahrah sucked in air, making her disapproving sound. 'She must tell him how it is,' she said. 'Not try and be sweet, like, Poor Scott, are you OK? You poor baby. Are you having a hard time? That's like giving him permission to continue. No. She must say, Scott, you got a problem and you're going to lose me, your friends and your chance of getting anywhere at school if you continue. Give it to him strong.'

'Probably easier said than done,' said Brook.

'It's the truth,' said Zahrah, 'and sometimes you have to be cruel to be kind.'

It had made me feel better talking to my mates about it all and I thought that each of them had given some good advice. 'I'll pass it all on,' I said. 'They both need help, her and Scott.'

'You tell her from me that she needs to be firm,' said Zahrah. 'My uncle used to drink and my aunt used to look after him like he was her baby and she was his mum. She'd clean him up, tell everybody that he wasn't really like the person he was when he was drunk. She was so sweet but like a doormat, you know.'

'What happened to them?' I asked.

'He cleaned up his act, gave up the drink, left my aunt and moved in with a woman who took no nonsense. I got the feeling that his being drunk gave my aunt a reason to live. She felt needed and, as long as he was messing up, she had him to look after and she didn't have to look at what was wrong with her own life.'

Wow, I thought. *Zahrah is so deep. She seems to have lived through a lot with her extended family.*

'Anyway, enough about me. What about you guys – what did you get up to while I was away?' I asked. 'Leela, didn't you have a second date with one of the boys from Portobello Road?'

Leela nodded then pulled an unhappy face. 'We had a great time on the first date. He was cute and fun. We really got along and then, on the second date, we went to the movies and he started up with the funny business which isn't so funny when you don't want it. His hand started creeping up my shirt. I slapped him off and he'd be OK for a while, then ten minutes later he'd start again, creeping up my thigh.'

'What did you do?' asked Brook.

'I poured my popcorn over him and left. It was a rubbish film anyway. He called and apologised, but he's history as far as I'm concerned.'

'You go, girl,' said Zahrah and high-fived her.

'I heard about a boy who made a hole in the bottom of his popcorn carton,' I said, 'and he unzipped his trousers and put his thing in it and, when his girlfriend leaned over and put her hand in the box, well, let's just say she got a bit more than popcorn.'

We all cracked up laughing. 'Ewww,' said Brook. 'That's so disgusting. Why are boys so stupid and obsessed with their things? They're always wanting to get them out and show them or get you to touch them and it's like, ewww . . .'

'Bruno wasn't like that,' I said.

'Give him time,' said Zahrah. 'Boys are all the same.'

'No, they're not,' said Leela. 'Some boys are nice and don't push their luck. I'm not going to let one bad experience put me off. I wasn't that into him anyway. Like, if I was, I might still have poured the popcorn over him but I might have talked about it with him afterwards. You know. Told him that I wasn't ready.'

'Most boys are cool if you tell them that although most will try it on too,' said Brook. 'You just have to let them know it's not on. How about you, Zahrah? How's it going with Ryan, your new lover boy?'

Zahrah raised an eyebrow. 'OK. We met on Saturday and mooched about bookshops, then went for coffee. Just getting to know each other really. He's nice and I think he knows not to try anything on or he'd regret it.'

Leela laughed. 'Yeah like imagine if anyone tried the thing in the popcorn box with you, you'd probably grab it and pull it until the boy yelped for help.'

'Or maybe accidentally on purpose I could pour hot coffee in there,' Zahrah said with a wicked grin.

'Ooooh,' the rest of us chorused.

'That's what he'd deserve if he tried a trick like that,' she said primly.

I felt a tad sorry for Ryan or indeed any boy that Zahrah went out with. When she did finally meet her match, he would have to be well tough to survive – she was a force to be reckoned with.

Although it was only Monday, I still felt on a high from the weekend. I'd told the girls every last detail of what had happened in Ravello which was great because it was like I'd got to relive the weekend and it feel real again. We had so much to tell each other and it felt as if we'd been apart loads – longer than just a weekend. We spent the whole lunch hour catching up on each other's news and how the love challenge was shaping up. So far, Zahrah and I were doing the best in that I had Bruno and she had Ryan, although she wasn't giving away as much as I was about what went on between them. Brook and Leela weren't put off by their lack of success though, because there was the party on Saturday night at Mikey's house and we were all invited. I confessed that I was hoping that there might have been a text or an email from Bruno but, after the poem, there had been no contact.

'Do you think I should text him?' I asked after we'd had everyone's news and I felt it would be OK to talk about Bruno again. (I didn't want to hog the stage and go on about it too much, although it was tempting.)

'No way. You mustn't,' said Zahrah. 'You don't want to appear too keen. Boys like the chase.'

'Yeah, maybe,' I said, 'but it wasn't like that with Bruno. That was what was so special. He wasn't like a lot of English boys, playing it cool. He was really into me and didn't mind who knew it.'

'I think it might be nice if you sent him a text to say thank you for his hospitality in showing you around,' said Brook. 'That's not being too keen, that's just good manners and it sounds like he took you to some gorgeous places and, of course, it opens up the way for him to reply.'

She didn't have to tell me twice because I agreed with her.

Mum always told us to write a card to say thank you if we'd been somewhere for dinner or lunch. It would be showing Bruno that I knew how to behave and it would be good for him to know that I had good manners for our future life together. As the bell for afternoon lessons went, I got out my phone and wrote a text:

Thanks for the poem, thanks for the weekend, thanks for being you.

I had already programmed his number into my phone in Italy before we left so I simply found it then pressed Send.

As we made our way to double maths, we passed Joe in the corridor.

He smiled when he saw me. 'Hey, Ruspoli, good weekend in Italy?'

'Fab,' I said. 'Scenery meeting go OK?'

'No probs,' Joe replied.

'She met the most divine boy in Italy,' interrupted Leela.

'And he's soooo handsome,' added Brook, 'like the most handsome boy in the whole of Italy.'

Zahrah moved her shoulder forward in a casual shrug and gave him a 'so there' look.

I pretended that I was embarrassed, but secretly I was chuffed that the girls had blurted out about Bruno. *You're not the only one who has other admirers,* I thought as Joe's expression became slightly troubled. He soon masked it, muttering, 'Cool, good for you,' as he went off down the corridor.

'Yeah, he is,' Zahrah called after him.

★ ★ ★

In the afternoon break, I checked my phone but there was no reply from Bruno.

'Oh God, maybe I was too gushy,' I groaned, clicking my phone shut.

'What did you write?' asked Zahrah.

'Thanks for the poem, thanks the weekend, thanks for being you.'

Zahrah sucked in air with disapproval.

'That's *so* sweet,' said Brook. 'Perfect.'

'He'll text back, don't worry,' said Leela. 'He's probably in a lecture or a meeting.'

'Yeah,' I said.

But he didn't text back.

Not that afternoon.

Nor that evening.

Nor the next day.

Nor the next.

It was so frustrating. Every part of me wanted to pick up the phone and call him, but I knew that I'd sound desperate if I did. Or accusing.

'You can't text him again,' said Leela when I told her on Friday that I still hadn't heard from him.

'But maybe it got wiped off his phone by mistake,' I said. 'I've done that sometimes, you know, deleted a message.'

Zahrah shook a finger at me. 'You know it didn't. Don't go there.'

'Maybe there's a problem with his provider,' I said. 'Or maybe someone stole his phone.'

'Other people have phones. He could have borrowed one,' said Zahrah.

'So *why* would he say that he'd call and then not?' I groaned.

'He's a boy,' said Zahrah.

'But he *wasn't* like other boys,' I moaned. 'He really wasn't. Something has happened. Maybe he had an accident and is lying . . . ohmigod, do you think I'd better phone to find out if he's all right?'

'India, chill. No way something has happened to him,' said Zahrah. 'He could still have called you. If any of those things had happened or all of them, he could easily have got your number, especially if your dad and his are such good friends.'

Brook shook her head sadly and gave me a hug. 'And you know the rules, India, you've texted him once. The ball's in his court now.'

I kicked the wall. I knew she was right. I could come up with all the excuses in the world for why he hadn't called but none of them washed. My new love had forgotten me the second my plane had taken off. *Love hurts*, I thought as we trooped out of the school gates and into the abyss of loneliness that was London on a dark evening in the rain.

Chapter 13

Tragic Heroine: Take Two

My plan for the weekend was to hide in my room, play sad music and be every inch one of the tragic heroine types that I'd decided not to be. I'd thought I was different. I'd thought *Bruno* and I were different but, no, I was just another love-sick fool and my love was unrequited. On Friday night after supper and a night flicking channels (every one of them seemed to show people in lu-urve), I couldn't sleep and part of my mind was urging me to call Bruno, to be adult about it and to just sort it out. He wasn't a game player. If we spoke, I could just find the solution to his silence. So I called his mobile.

I got put through to voicemail and hearing his lovely accent made me feel all gooey inside. 'Hi . . . it's India . . . oh shit!' I didn't know what to say. 'Oh er . . . never mind, sorry, wrong number.' *Oh bollards,* I thought when I clicked my phone shut. *That was really really stupid. I should have planned what message I wanted to leave. And now I really do sound desperate and oh noooooooooooo, he'll know it was me. Arghhhhhhh.* I longed to talk to one of my friends about it, but I knew that the girls would be mad with me if they knew I'd phoned. I was mad with myself. I wouldn't tell them. And I certainly wouldn't tell Erin. She'd go ballistic. Even in the midst of her own troubles, she'd find time to remind me of the rules about boys – Number one: don't get desperate – and calling a boy in the middle of the night surely counts as very desperate. Super desperate. *Oh arghhhhhhhhhhhhhh.*

On Saturday, I told Mum that I wasn't taking any calls unless it was Bruno, then I went and sat with my mobile at my window for ages and stared down at the wet streets below. The occasional person hurried by under their umbrella. I gazed up at the sky and clouds and thought, *He may be in Italy and I may be here in England, but it's the same sky that covers us both and somewhere he's under it, maybe even looking up from wherever he is.*

I stared at my phone and willed it to ring.

It didn't.

I called our landline from my mobile to check that it was working, and then regretted it because that might have been the very moment that Bruno was trying to get through on either of the phones (I had given him both numbers).

I stared at my mobile and the landline phone and willed them to ring.

They didn't.

The words that Dad had quoted in the car on the way back from the airport played over in my mind: 'Time is too slow for those who wait . . .' *But he could have left a message on my voicemail,* said my inner voice that I call Sensible Sadie. (I have three inner voices: Sensible Sadie, Paranoid Penny and Wimpy Wanda. They come out when I'm super-stressed and Sensible Sadie talks such common sense it makes me even more stressed.)

You've blown it now, idiot, said Paranoid Penny. *You look soooo desperate.*

I'm such a loser, all boys hate me, said Wimpy Wanda.

Oh shut up, I told them all, but I couldn't help feeling that I was, just like Ophelia, a thoroughbred tragic misery. *I shall waste away and people will find my bones and, when they bury me, word will get to Bruno and he'll come to the funeral and everyone will be crying and then he'll be sorry,* I thought. *He'll know it was his fault and be guilty for the rest of his life and I'll be glad. In fact, I'll haunt him and, if he ever falls in love with a girl and tries to kiss her, I'll pull her hair and tweak his elbows and make his life a misery.*

There was a timid knock on my door. 'India, it's Mum. Are you going to come down?' She poked her head around the door.

'I can't, Mum. I can't face anyone. How can I come down and be with the rest of you when my life is over?'

'Still no word?'

'Nothing.'

Mum came and sat on the end of the bed. 'You're still young, India. There will be others.'

'*Nooooooo*,' I moaned. 'You don't understand. I don't *want* there to be others. I only wanted *him*. *He* was probably my *soul*mate.' I felt my eyes fill with tears. I bit them back. 'I hate boys. I *really* do. They *so* mess your head up.'

Mum reached out and took my hand. 'Yes, they do but only some of the time. Don't give up yet, India, I'm sure there's an explanation. And if there isn't, well you have to let him go. There are lots of nice boys out there. What about that lovely boy who brought you home the other week? He was nice.'

'No he wasn't. He hasn't called either. I was thinking about him today. There was me all worried that I hadn't got his number to call and thank him, but he knows where I live. He brought me back here. So why didn't he call round to see how I was? If he liked me, he could have got in touch. Why does it have to be me who does all the chasing? It's soooo not fair.'

Mum squeezed my hand. 'It won't always be you, India. The right boy will come along and you won't know what hit you.'

'I thought Bruno *was* the right boy but look at me. It's the weekend and I'm on my own —'

'I thought Mikey was having a party. That's tonight, isn't it? There will be boys there.'

'Not ones that I want. The ones I want don't want me. What's wrong with me?'

The corners of Mum's mouth twitched slightly like she was going to laugh, but she caught herself just in time and made her expression serious and concerned. 'Nothing's wrong with you. You're a lovely, kind and beautiful girl. And I'm not just saying that because I'm your mother. The right boy will come along. Don't put the walls up. Not yet.'

Inside I felt all mixed up. I was bored sitting in my room being miserable – normally I'm not a depressed type of person. And I was starting to get hungry. I hadn't eaten since breakfast. As always Mum picked up on my thoughts.

'I've done a shepherd's pie just the way you like it with cheese on top of the mash. Everyone's downstairs. Lewis and Ethan . . .'

'Is there pudding?'

'Damson crumble.'

My stomach started to rumble. 'With custard?'

'And vanilla ice cream.'

'I suppose I'd better eat something.'

Mum smiled. 'I think you ought to and . . .'

'What?'

'Leela and Brook both called. They said they'd come by to pick you up around seven to go over to Zahrah's to get ready for Mikey's party.'

'I told them I wasn't going.'

'I know. Leela told me. She said to tell you that she's coming to collect you anyway.'

'She's very bossy.'

'I know. I like her. So, have a bit of food and go out and enjoy yourself. So Bruno hasn't been in touch? You know what the best revenge is?'

'What?'

116

'To live well. Go out and have a good time.'

I stared at the picture of him. 'You know what. I will. Just give me a moment. I have to do something.'

Mum got up. 'OK. See you in five then.'

I nodded. I waited until she had left the room, then I got my scissors out, picked up the photo of me and Bruno and cut it into a hundred tiny pieces. 'There, that's what I think of you,' I said, letting the pieces fall into the bin. 'Now where's that stupid poem you sent because that's going in the bin as well.'

I cut up the poem and took a deep breath. *Onwards,* I told myself. *I'm going to go out and make boys fall in love with me, but I shall be aloof and unobtainable and break* their *hearts for a change. That's what I'll do.*

I went downstairs, had a great supper and a laugh with my family. Then I went back upstairs, put on the rust-coloured silk dress that I'd worn in Italy, blow-dried my hair until it looked super glossy, did my nails and waited for the girls.

The doorbell rang and Mum called up the stairs that Leela and Brook had arrived.

I checked my appearance in the mirror and looked out of the window up at the clouds.

'Your loss, Bruno,' I said to the sky.

Chapter 14

Party-time

'I hope he's invited the neighbours,' said Brook when we got to the road where the party was being held. We could hear the music pounding already.

We made our way to the door where a crowd of teenagers were standing in the garden and Mikey's mum and dad were crossing off names on a guest list. Zahrah spotted Ryan standing on his own opposite the house and waved. He came over to join us and we manoeuvred our way through the crowd, gave our names and were ushered inside.

'We're with them,' said a girl's voice behind us.

'Is that right, India?' asked Mr Davidson. I turned to see a blonde girl who was frantically nodding at me and, for a second, I panicked because I didn't know what to do. 'Er . . .'

'You go on in, India,' said Mr Davidson and he turned back

to the girl. 'Listen. I've told you, if you're not on the list, you can't come in.'

Mickey came out of the kitchen at the back of the house. 'Hey, you made it,' he said, helping me off with my coat. 'Put your stuff upstairs in the bedroom on the left.'

'What's going on, Mikey?' asked Leela. 'Who are all the people outside?'

'Gatecrashers,' he replied. 'The girls are the worst – they're so pushy.'

'I'd have thought you'd have let spare girls in, knowing you,' I said.

Mikey grinned. 'I checked them out first, don't worry, but Dad was very firm. If they're not on the list, they don't come in. I think Mum and Dad are nervous – they've heard so many bad things about teenage parties.'

'It's probably not a bad idea not to let people in if you don't know them,' said Zahrah as Ryan helped her off with her coat. I was surprised to see that she let him do it – Zahrah is usually so independent and it was unusual to see her acting girlie. She was wearing an ivory T-shirt, a long amber necklace and earrings, a brown ruff skirt that barely covered her bum, dark tights and knee-length suede boots. She'd applied more make-up than I'd ever seen her wear before and she looked stunning.

Mikey looked her up and down. 'Wow Zahrah, you look amazing,' he said, and Ryan put his arm around her as if to say, Yeah and she's with me. Mikey got the message and turned to face Brook, Leela and me. 'In fact, you all do.'

We dutifully did a twirl for him. It was good to have our efforts appreciated. We'd spent ages at Zahrah's house, crammed into the small room that she shared with her sister Aisha. We'd swapped jewellery, helped each other with our make-up and tried on loads of each other's clothes before we all settled on what we were wearing. I had on my silk dress with a hip belt over skinny jeans with my cowboy boots and ropes of Zahrah's brown and cream shell necklaces. Brook looked divine in a steel-grey Charleston dress that was pure vintage, which her mother had picked up in a boutique in Greenwich Village last time they were in New York, and Leela was wearing black trousers and a black silk halter-neck that she'd borrowed from Brook. She looked really sophisticated.

Ryan and Zahrah offered to get drinks and, as soon as they'd gone, Mikey pulled me into the corner and beckoned Leela and Brook to come with us.

'You haven't forgotten your promise, have you?' he asked. 'The snog lesson?'

'But what about Amy?' I asked. 'She's not going to like it if she sees you kissing four strange girls.'

'Amy couldn't make it. It's her brother's twenty-first tonight and she couldn't get out of it,' he said. Then he made his lips pucker. 'So ready when you are.'

'Later,' said Leela. 'First we have to check out the talent.'

'But you promised,' said Mikey.

'The night is young,' said Leela, and she pulled Brook and me towards the back of the hall. 'And the girls and I have things to do.'

Mikey stuck his bottom lip out.

'Later,' said Leela. 'Promise.'

He slouched off to join his parents, who were still fending off unwelcome guests. Once he was out of earshot, Leela leaned towards Brook and me. 'OK, let's split up and have a look around. Check out who's here. Meet in the kitchen in . . . say, half an hour to discuss step two. Synchronise watches.'

We checked our watches to see that we all had the same time and then Leela went upstairs, Brook into the front room and I went into the back. I began the casual 'Oh I'm looking for someone I know' scan while taking in the boys there and which ones were in a couple and which were single. My heart sank when my glance reached the left corner, for there was Joe with a stunningly pretty petite blonde girl in a short black dress. She had her hand up on his shoulder and was laughing at something he had said. I felt such a stab of jealousy. It hit me before I could tell myself that I didn't care about him any more. He saw me looking and waved. The girl looked over at me too. She didn't look very friendly so I decided not to go and talk to them. Besides, he might have asked me about my new Italian boyfriend we'd boasted about on Monday. *Arghhhhh, I hate you Bruno*, I thought for the hundredth time that week. Just at that moment, Eddie O'Neil cornered me and slipped his arm around me. Out of the corner of my eye, I could see Joe watching from the other side of the room so I gave Eddie my full attention, and within minutes, he went for the snog. I didn't resist because I wanted Joe to see that I wasn't pining over him. Eddie put his lips on mine, opened his mouth and started moving his head around. The kiss felt very sloppy and all wrong. And then he stuck his tongue right into my mouth and started sloshing it around. It made me think of a washing machine on rinse cycle. It was horrible, too wet with saliva, and I stepped back as soon as I could. Eddie tried to pull me back to him but I shook my head.

'That was just an early Christmas kiss,' I said so as not to hurt his feelings.

'How about another for New Year?' he asked.

Over my dead body, I thought. 'Er . . . maybe closer to the time,' I said as I headed for the cloakroom in the hall, feeling a sudden need to wash my face. I didn't care if Joe had seen me pull away from Eddie. I wasn't going to do dog-slobber kissing, not even to make Joe jealous.

Half an hour was almost up, so I checked back in the kitchen but none of my mates were in there. I went back into the hall where Mr and Mrs Davidson seemed to be having a hard time holding back a crowd of teenagers who were doing everything they could to get in and Mr Davidson was pushing the door closed with all his might. Seconds later, there was the sound of glass smashing in the front room, a scream and everyone came running out into the hall, a shaken-looking Brook included.

'That's it. I'm going to call the police,' said Mr Davidson. 'I'm not having any more of this. Mikey! Where's Mikey?'

Mikey came out of the front room with a boy who had a cut on his forehead and was looking very pale. 'Someone threw something. I think it was a brick,' said Mikey.

Mrs Davidson rushed forward and ushered the boy to sit on one of the stairs. Mr Davidson opened the door and shouted out into the street, 'Police are on their way.' And then he slammed the door and made the phone call.

I put my arm around Brook. 'You OK?' I asked.

She nodded. 'Yeah. I think. They're not from our school, are they?'

'I didn't recognise anyone when I came in,' I said.

Mikey peered through the hall window. 'They seem to be going, Dad,' he said.

Mr Davidson looked angry. 'Good,' he said. 'Never again, I tell you. Never again. We shouldn't have had the party this time. I've a good mind to go out there and thump the lot of them.'

Mrs Davidson's back stiffened. 'Don't be an idiot,' she said. 'You do that and you'll be the one that ends up in prison. Let the police deal with it. Besides, these days, you never know who's carrying a knife.'

Mr Davidson shook his head. 'Little buggers,' he said. 'It's all wrong you know. All wrong.'

'I'm taking Matt to casualty,' said Mrs Davidson, looking at the boy with the cut. 'Now you hold the fort here while I'm out and, for heaven's sake, don't do anything stupid and don't let anyone else in.'

'Looks like they've all gone,' said Mikey from his viewpoint by the window. 'It should be all right now.'

The police arrived about half an hour later, by which time the crowd outside had disappeared. Everyone was talking about what had happened; it was like we'd all been given an almighty shot of adrenalin and from then on, the party took off and people were dancing, chatting, laughing and letting off steam.

'Great party,' said Leela when I finally got to meet up with her and Brook in the kitchen. 'So how goes it with my team?'

Brook sighed. 'No joy. Three boys, three rejects,' she said. She held up the first finger. 'One was just about OK, Martin, dark hair, nice smile. We got chatting and then I took him some food. Ee-yuk. He ate with his mouth open. Disgusting.' She held up the next finger. 'Second guy, Josh, cute but had bad breath.' She held up the third finger. 'Third guy was from our school. He's sweet – Oliver, and I know that he fancies me. I actually let him kiss me but he kept his mouth so tight closed and gave me kisses like an old aunt would give you, you know, light pecks. Like he didn't know how to join them up into a proper kiss.'

'Sounds like a pigeon,' said Leela and made her neck go back and forth like pigeons do.

'But where are boys supposed to learn how to be good kissers?' I asked. 'Maybe you should have persevered, Brook, and shown him how to do it.'

'I don't think so,' said Brook. 'If you like him, *you* teach him. He's in the front room last time I saw him, trying to get off with Mary Camberwell from Year Ten. No. I know what I want, he's not here tonight and I'm not going to compromise. What about you, Leela?'

'No result. I spent some time with Greg from Year Twelve, but he is so boring, droning on about the best route to get here and the best route to get to school. He looks good, but who cares when his company sends you to sleep. And I spent about half a minute with Tony Johnson, but he's such a creep, like, trying to get his hands up my top. He just doesn't get it. He is never going to get off with anyone unless he learns to at least have a conversation before he tries the fumbly stuff.'

'No one else?' I asked.

Leela shook her head. 'How've you got on, India?' she asked.

'Eddie O'Neil did the dog slobber,' I said, 'and that's the sum total of my success.'

Leela looked at me sympathetically. 'I saw Joe with Katie Morrison.'

'Who is she?' I asked.

'She's in the Lower Sixth,' said Brook.

'I've never noticed her,' I murmured.

'Are you OK?' asked Leela.

'Oh yeah. I am so over him,' I replied. I saw Leela and Brook exchange a glance and added, 'I am. I really am.'

''Course you are,' said Leela, 'and if it's any consolation, I just heard him having a row with Katie upstairs outside the bathroom. I don't think they knew I was in there. But of course, if you're over him, you probably don't care what was said . . .'

I narrowed my eyes. 'Did I ever tell you that one of my talents is the ancient art of giving Chinese burns?' I said as I reached out to grab her wrist.

Leela laughed and hid her arms behind her back. 'No. You didn't but your brother Dylan did.'

'So spill,' I said. 'Or you will regret it. Although I am only interested from a purely academic point of view.'

'Yeah sure,' said Brook. 'We believe you.'

'So?' I asked Leela.

'Katie was saying that she wanted more of a commitment from Joe,' she replied, 'and he was saying that he thought that part of the reason that they'd got together was because neither of them wanted to feel tied down.'

'Hah, that's the line he gave me,' I said.

'Anyway,' said Leela. 'She was saying that her feelings for him have changed and that she wanted a proper relationship or nothing at all.'

'Wow,' I said. 'I bet he didn't like that!'

'What did he say?' asked Brook.

'He said that he wasn't going to lie to her and that he couldn't guarantee that, and he didn't want to set something up then let her down. And she said then, in that case, he couldn't feel that strongly about her.'

'I saw her leave about ten minutes ago,' said Brook. 'I thought she looked upset.'

'Hey, anyone seen Zahrah?' asked Leela.

Brook nodded. 'She and Ryan are hogging the sofa in the back room.'

'Yeah, I saw them too,' I said. 'Having a snogathon.'

'She really likes him, doesn't she?' said Leela. 'I've never seen her like this. Maybe we should go and crawl behind the sofa and jump out and scare them.'

'Nah,' said Brook. 'Leave them alone.'

I nodded gloomily. 'Yeah because it probably won't last.'

'Oh I don't know,' said Brook. 'I've never seen Zahrah so smitten before. I'd give them at least a few weeks.'

At that moment, Mikey spotted us from the hall, grinned, came into the kitchen and closed the door. 'OK, ladies, time to tango, I do believe.'

Leela laughed. 'You ready for this?'

Mikey nodded and, without giving him a second to draw breath, Leela went straight over to him and snogged him. After a few minutes, she stepped back and Mikey did a fake swoon, let his knees buckle and slid to the floor with a silly smile on his face.

Leela stood over him. 'Get up,' she said. 'We're not done with you yet. Now that was the spontaneous I-can't-resist-you-type kiss. Brook, you're on next.'

Dutifully, Mikey stood up. Brook stepped forward, took his hands and put them around her neck and snogged him. When she moved away, he put his hand on his heart and grinned.

'That was a romantic-type kiss,' said Brook. 'Slower, softer. OK?'

Mikey nodded. 'I *like* this but I think I need a *lot* more practice. Um. Who's next? Oh yeah. You, India.'

'I'm all snogged out,' I said, 'but I will give you some hints. Don't open your mouth too much. Don't keep it tight closed either. You want it sort of in between and relaxed. Don't shove your tongue in her mouth straight away. Wait a while before you do tongue kissing. Build up to it and then press in gently and take your lead from her. If she puts hers forward then you can nudge it a bit. Try it on the back of your hand. Also, if your tongue is too floppy and out of control, it feels messy and too wet, like you're kissing a live fish. Keep a little control of your tongue, it feels nicer. Try it out.'

'Show me,' said Mikey.

I put my hand up to my mouth and kissed it.

Mikey sighed. 'Not like that. It's not fair, India Jane. You promised to show me. Just *show* me.'

'Yeah,' said Leela. 'Me and Brook both did and it *is* his birthday.'

'It is my birthday,' Mikey repeated.

The three of them were standing looking at me in such a pleading way that, in the end, I pulled Mikey to me and kissed him. It was a nice gentle kiss. I stepped away. 'That was fine, Mikey, you have nothing to be worried about, but you want to know the real secret of a good kiss?'

Mikey nodded.

'Chemistry,' I said. 'It makes it all fizz.'

'OK,' said Mikey, then he smiled. 'Want to go again?'

I shook my head. Behind me, the door opened and someone came in. I turned to see Joe. 'All right guys?' he asked. We all looked at the floor, suddenly embarrassed and silent, and Mikey shuffled out. 'What's going on? You're looking strange. India?'

'Oh nothing – just talking about the weather, weren't we?' I blustered.

'Yes. Um. Cold out, isn't it?' said Brook.

Joe laughed and shook his head as if he didn't believe a word of it. 'You girls,' he said, helping himself to a can of lager.

Brook manoeuvred herself behind Joe, looked at Leela and jerked her chin towards the door as if to say, Let's go. Leela stared at her as if she was mad for a second and then she got it. 'Oh. Right. Yeah. Hey, need the loo. Come with me Brook, yeah?'

'I'll come with you,' I said. I didn't want to be left alone with Joe, no matter what my friends thought.

'No, no, you stay here,' said Brook. 'Besides I need to talk to Leela about something.' And they both disappeared.

Joe raised an eyebrow. 'Subtle, hey?' he said. 'I get the feeling that they wanted to leave us alone.'

'I've no idea why,' I said, and I knew that it came out sounding really snooty. Joe hid a smile, which annoyed me, so I decided to annoy him back. 'So where's your new girlfriend?'

Joe shrugged a shoulder. 'She wasn't really my girlfriend,' he said, then he grinned. 'She's stormed off. Think I upset her, but . . . I was only being honest.'

I decided to pretend that I didn't know what Leela had told me and to play innocent instead. 'Why, what did you do?'

'More like what I didn't do. I don't know, India. You know me. You know what I'm like.'

'Not really,' I said. I turned and looked into his eyes and I felt all the old chemistry. I knew that he was feeling it too because he smiled again but in a knowing way. It made my toes curl.

Joe leaned against the washing machine and took a swig of his drink. 'I wish I knew what I wanted.'

'What do you mean? In life? In relationships? What?'

'Girls,' he said. 'Like, I've been trying to play it really straight

129

this term, you know, on the level, telling the truth so that no one can label me a rat or whatever. Seems it backfires though. Now Kate hates me and probably you do too.'

'Not hate exactly,' I said.

Joe laughed and I laughed back to show I meant it as a joke, even though I wasn't sure that I did. I felt mixed up about what I felt. Like, how could I feel something as strong as I had last weekend for Bruno and, hardly a week later, be feeling the same for Joe, who I thought I was over? *Not that either of them wants me,* I thought as another flash of frustration went through me. *Two kisses with boys that I don't fancy and the ones that I do fancy, don't want to know. It's sooooooo annooooooooying!*

Joe looked at me closely. I so wished that he didn't have such beautiful eyes with such long curly eyelashes. And I wished he didn't have such a lovely bottom lip, plump and just pulling me to kiss it. I remembered when we had kissed. It had been delicious. His lips were like a soft silk cushion. *But he doesn't want you,* I told myself.

'What then?' he asked.

'What then what?'

'What if it's not exactly hate?'

'Why do you want to know what I feel?' I blurted. 'You're just playing with me because Katie has gone.'

Joe looked surprised. 'I . . . I . . .' he stuttered and for a second I regretted sounding so cross with him. *But boys are a pain,* I thought, stomping off to find Leela and Brook.

Chapter 15

Post-mortem

'I think he still likes you,' said Leela as she pulled her duvet up to her chin. Brook, Zahrah and I were having a sleepover at her house after the party. Brook was in the pull-out bed on the other side of the room to Leela's and Zahrah and I were on an inflatable mattress on the floor. We'd had mugs of hot chocolate with cinnamon sprinkled on top and Leela's auntie had plied us with delicious little Indian sweets with pistachios, cardamon and honey. I was feeling stuffed and a half – I love them and had eaten twice as many as anyone else.

'I do too,' said Brook. 'You can tell by the way he looks at you – like with a half smile.

'I know that look. I don't think it means anything apart from the fact that he thinks I'm barking mad. I always seem to say the wrong thing when I'm with him.'

'A sign of true love,' Brook declared.

'No it's not. For true love, surely both people have to feel it.' I didn't want to talk about Joe any more. It made me cross. And frustrated. He was a waste of space. And so was Bruno. Thinking about him made me even crosser. 'I really really really am off boys. I tried. It didn't work out. End of story.'

'I don't think you should give up,' said Zahrah. 'Maybe it's just that they're not the boys for you. Someone better will come along.'

Brook and Leela sat up and stared at Zahrah.

'What?' she asked. 'Why are you gawping at me?'

'Because we've never ever heard you talk like that. You're the Queen of Cynicism,' said Leela.

'Yeah,' said Brook.

Zahrah smiled. 'Well you never know what or who is around the next corner. Plus I am in love. Yes. Me. L-ove.'

'That's so fantastic!' said Brook. 'I thought you were keen on Ryan but love? That's top.'

'Yeah,' said Leela.

'Yes,' I said. 'I'm really pleased for you.'

Zahrah glanced at my face and cracked up. 'Looks like it. I've never seen anyone with such a long face.'

I made an effort to smile and to lighten up and be enthusiastic for her, but when Leela turned the light off and we snuggled down, my uncomfortable mood settled back on me like a bad haircut. *Such a lot has happened*, I thought. *Like, life goes around in circles. Good, bad, good, bad. First I was mugged. Then I had the most romantic weekend of my whole life in Ravello. Then back to a week of misery. First Joe, then Tyler, then Bruno. Three boys and yet I'm no closer to having an actual boyfriend.* As I lay there looking up at the ceiling, I decided that I was going to forget about boys, no matter what my friends said. I was just going to get on with life. Carry on with my school life and forget about Leela's challenge and looking for the perfect boy. If he was out there, he could come looking for me. The other way round was doing my head in.

After a big breakfast of mango lassies in Leela's mum's fab modern kitchen, I got home at around eleven and went to my room to catch up on homework. First though I wanted to contact Erin – it felt like ages since I had spoken to her. Sadly, she wasn't at home and her mobile was off so, with no excuses left, I turned my mobile off and got stuck into painting a design for panels for one of the scenes in the school show. After a couple of hours, I heard the front door bell ring. Five minutes later, Aunt Sarah called up the stairs. 'India. Come and see.'

I went down the stairs and Aunt Sarah was standing in the hallway with the most stunning bunch of flowers and a small silver box with a red bow on it.

'For you,' she said with a big smile and held them out. 'Looks like you have an admirer.'

'But who?'

Aunt Sarah pulled a little card from the flowers. '*To my Cinnamon Girl,*' she read. 'Oh, isn't that romantic?'

The flowers were a mix of hyacinth and freesias and they

smelled divine. And the little parcel looked like it might be some fab Belgian chocolates.

Aunt Sarah turned over the card. '*Bruno,*' she read.

'*Bruno?*'

'Bruno.'

I felt the hard wall I had built around myself to keep everyone out crumble and fall as delight flooded through me. He hadn't forgotten me after all. 'But . . .'

'Shall I put them in water for you?' asked Aunt Sarah.

'Oh yes. No. I'll do it. Thanks.'

I took the bouquet from her and went to find a vase, my mind was reeling with possibilities. What had happened?

I didn't have to wait long because, when I went back upstairs with the flowers, I turned my mobile on to see if there were any messages from Erin and it bleeped that I had two. One was a text from Erin saying that she was home and would be waiting on MSN and one was a voicemail message from Bruno.

'*Bella,*' he said. 'I've been trying to reach you all week. I was studying in Positano the week after you'd gone and I lost my phone there. I left it in a restaurant and, when I went back, it was gone. And getting hold of your grandmother was a nightmare. She never answers her calls, but I kept trying and at last got through and oh . . . this sounds like a lot of excuses but, India, you know how it was with us. Please call me. I need to hear your voice. More than that. I need to see your lovely face. I am coming over next weekend and hope to see you again then. Call me.'

I felt stunned. I sat down and switched on the computer to contact Erin on MSN. I had to tell her my news before calling Bruno. As I pressed the computer keys, I heard the door bell ring again and, once again, Aunt Sarah called me down. This time, she had a bunch of white roses and a larger card than the last one. 'Not more from Bruno?' I asked.

Once again, Aunt Sarah looked at the card. 'No. It says . . . sure you want me to read this?'

I nodded.

'It says, *Sorry I'm a fool who can't commit. Doesn't mean I don't rate you. Meet me after school on Tuesday at Costa. I will try and explain. From You Know Who.* Do you know who?' she asked.

I nodded again. Joe. 'I'll get a vase,' I said.

I took the flowers, put them in a vase then went back upstairs and placed Joe's flowers next to Bruno's on my desk. Jut looking at them made me smile. *Just wait until I tell Erin*, I thought as I typed my way into MSN.

Cinnamongirl: You there?

Irishbrat4eva: Yeah.

Cinnamongirl: Sorry, sorry, but you'll never guess what's been happening. I have loads to tell you.

Irishbrat4eva: Me too.

Cinnamongirl: You go first.

Irishbrat4eva: No, you . . .

Cinnamongirl: No, you. Is there more news about Scott?

Irishbrat4eva: Yeah. I sent him a letter.

Cinnamongirl: Wow. What did you say?

Irishbrat4eva: I decided that, despite my mates over here saying to stay out of it, I couldn't. I had to do something. I couldn't stand back and see someone I care about ruin their life so I sent him a letter saying that, if he ever needed anyone to talk to, I was there for him.

Cinnamongirl: Did he reply?

Irishbrat4eva: Not a word. Did I do the wrong thing do you think?

Cinnamongirl: Not at all. You followed your heart. You care and sometimes that's all you can do in situations like this – just say, hey I'm still your friend. The rest has got to come from him. You can't make him stop drinking or smoking.

'INDIA,' Aunt Sarah's voice called up the stairs.

Cinnamongirl: Aunt Sarah's calling me.

Irishbrat4eva: No worries. I've got to go anyway – homework to catch up on. Just wanted to know what you thought.

Cinnamongirl: I think you did the right thing and he's lucky to have you as a friend. Later, hey?

Irishbrat4eva: Later.

I leapt back down the stairs two at a time and arrived with a thump at the bottom. 'More flowers?' I asked.

Aunt Sarah was making a strange face and jerking her chin towards the living room.

'So many admirers, so little time,' I said in my fake actor luvvie voice.

Aunt Sarah gave an exasperated sigh and jerked her thumb towards the living room. 'In there,' she said.

'Who?'

A tall handsome boy stepped into the hall.

Tyler.

My jaw fell open. 'Ohmigod, it's you!' I said. I turned to Aunt Sarah. 'This is Tyler. He's the boy who brought me home that day I was mugged.'

'Pleased to meet you, Tyler,' said Aunt Sarah. 'Now, India, remember your manners and show Tyler back into the living room and I'll bring you some drinks.'

'Oh. Right. Yeah.'

'Coffee or tea?' asked Aunt Sarah.

'Coffee. Black please,' Tyler replied.

Aunt Sarah disappeared and I stood rooted to the spot staring at Tyler. My mind had gone blank and my legs seemed to have frozen. Tyler was looking at me, waiting for me to say something. 'Oh yeah, um, come through,' I said finally and led him into the living room.

'I wanted to see how you were doing,' said Tyler.

'Me too. I mean . . . I wanted to see you again too – to thank you. I . . . I was in a daze that day. I can't even remember what I said or how we got home hardly.'

Tyler sat on the sofa and crossed his legs. I couldn't help but notice that he had a cat-like grace about him, very at ease in his body.

'Understandable after what had happened. You don't have to thank me,' he said. 'I just did what anyone would have done.'

'So where have you been then?' I blurted. 'I mean, I don't mean that in a demanding kind of way, I . . . oh, this is coming out all wrong. I mean, why have you waited until now to come round?'

'I only got back yesterday. I've been in New York. Remember I told you I want to do journalism? My uncle got me some work experience there. I was leaving the night you got mugged, which is why I had to go immediately after I'd brought you home. I was so preoccupied in getting you back safe and then getting home and then to the airport in time to make my flight I totally forgot to get your phone number so I could call to check up on you.'

'Wow. You were very chilled for someone who had a plane to catch.'

Tyler shrugged. 'Sometimes you have to go with what's in front of you,' he said and flashed me a wide flirty smile.

I felt myself blush. 'Well here you are now,' I said. 'I'm so glad you came round. Work experience in New York? That sounds fab. Tell me all about it.' I wanted to get him talking so that I could look at him properly. Brown eyes. Cheek bones to die for. A gorgeous sensuous mouth. And he looked toned, like he worked out.

'It was ace,' said Tyler. 'I'd love to tell you all about it but how about a bit later this afternoon? I know I've just arrived out of the blue and butted my way in – your Aunt Sarah was very cagey when she saw me at the door. So would it possible to meet up some place away from here and get to know each other properly?' When he said that he looked directly into my eyes and I felt myself blush even more.

'Er . . . yes, that would be great,' I said.

Boys really are like buses, I thought. *No one for ages then three come along all at once!*

Chapter 16

Raining Men

I needed to consult the committee.

As soon as Tyler had gone, I dashed upstairs and got on the phone. I felt so confused. Tyler. Bruno. Joe. What was going on? I tried Erin first, but her mum told me that she'd just gone out on an errand. Next I called Leela.

'What am I going to do?' I asked her after I'd filled her in. 'Which boy should I choose?'

'Bruno. Stick with Bruno,' she said. 'He's The One for you. I remember what a high you were on when you came back from Ravello. And you did say he might be your soulmate.'

She was right. But that had been before Joe had sent the roses. And before Tyler had got in touch. But it had been so lovely to get Bruno's flowers and get the message that he would be over the next weekend. Hearing his voice had brought back the wonderful time that I'd spent with him in Italy. But then . . . Tyler was such interesting company and so handsome – but more than that, there was something about him, like he viewed the world with a quiet intelligence and calm. It would be a shame not to spend some time with him. There was no guarantee that things were going to work out with Bruno and the fact that he lived in Italy was always going to cause some problems. And Joe. What about him? I knew that Joe and I had a connection but he was always on about not wanting to be tied down. It would be a pity not to explore what might be there with Tyler in the hope that Joe might come through, only to be let down by him again. Or had he changed his mind and begun to see that we really did have something special? God, it was difficult.

'What should I do?' I asked Brook after I'd hung up from talking to Leela.

'Joe, definitely,' she said. 'He's always been The One for you and you know it. You've been into him ever since your summer in Greece and now maybe he's beginning to realise it too. It was always a matter of time. I really believe that these things are never one way. And OK, so Bruno is probably lovely but you have to be practical and face facts, India – he lives in Italy. A long distance love affair. They never last.'

'Hmm. That's what I was thinking too,' I said.

I felt sad after we'd hung up. She was right about the distance, but it had felt so special with Bruno especially now I knew that he had been feeling the same as I had all along. Maybe there would be a way around it.

I called Zahrah.

'What should I do?' I asked.

'No contest,' she replied. 'Tyler. You were looking for a hero and he came through for you. He's the one with the least complications. Bruno lives abroad and, yes, there are phones and email but you can't snog in cyberspace. Joe doesn't know what he wants and has messed you about already and would do it again if you give him half a chance. He's not ready yet. So it has to be contestant number three. Tyler.'

'Tyler. Oh right,' I said. 'Thank you very much.'

After I'd hung up, I realised that I felt more confused than ever. Luckily Erin called soon after and I was able to put my question to her.

'Woah. I wish all decisions were so difficult,' she said when I'd finished telling her about the three boys. 'Hmm. Gorgeous boy one, two or three?'

'I know. It's like it's raining men over here.'

'Lucky you. It's raining water over here. I just got soaked when I went out. But you . . . How fab. Sounds like you got the hat-trick. Three in one.'

'Yeah but now I am so confused. Reeling. Bruno. Joe. Tyler. All in one afternoon. Why, oh why does it have to be like this? Nothing and then they all come at once.'

'What exactly did Bruno say on the message?'

'He was so sweet and apologetic. I can't think why I ever doubted him. And he said that he's coming over next weekend on business.'

'And Joe?'

'He just sent the flowers. No promises or proposals, but he suggested we meet up next week – kind of casual.'

'Hmm. But sounds like an opening of sorts. A maybe. And what about Tyler?'

'He asked me out later this afternoon.'

'So are you going to go?'

'Yes, I think so. For one thing, I owe him one for coming to my rescue that day and it might not be a date date. Just coffee and getting to know each other.'

'OK. This is what you do. No harm in postponing your decision. You see what happens. You don't have to decide this exact moment. Go out with Tyler, see if there's anything there. Go out with Joe too – or at least meet up with him next week. See what he says and if there is anything still there. And when Bruno is over, spend time with him. Decide later when you're clearer about how you feel.'

'But would I be being unfaithful to any of them? I'd hate to hurt anyone.'

'Are you engaged to be married to any of them?'

'No. 'Course not but, if we heard about a boy seeing three girls, we'd all think he was a total love rat – and now I'm doing it.'

'Yeah. I see what you mean. Like it's OK for you but not for a boy.'

'Sort of. But I am not a love rat. I didn't set out for any of this to happen.'

'OK. So chill. It's early days. You're not even going out with any of them, are you? It's not like any of them really sees you as their girlfriend.'

'Not exactly . . . maybe Bruno does a bit.'

'Yeah but he lives in Italy. Listen. Go with the flow. That's my advice. Decide later. And until you snog Tyler, you won't really know if there is chemistry.'

Just thinking about snogging Tyler made me feel funny so I had no doubt the real thing would be fab.

'You are very wise, O lady from the green land,' I said.

'Oh yeah, we've forgotten our Shakespeare-speak lately, haven't we? Well, get thee on some dates fair maid and let thy heart speak its own desire.'

'Verily I will. So what about yon naughty knight of the realm, Sir Scott? He that dost sup till stupor on yon ale?'

'I have decided to try a zen approach since we spoke earlier and that is to let him be. Let myself be. Let the universe be.'

'Cool. And if that doesn't work what else are you going to do?'

'Not sure. Witchcraft maybe. Wait until the next full moon. Cut off some of his toenails while he's asleep, put them in a bowl, a bit of slug and a few herbs and do a spell.'

'Sounds as good a plan as any and at least you sound happier than this morning.'

'Exactly. I was thinking about what you said. It has to come from him. I've done what I can and sometimes there is time for a plan. Other times not. This week we let the universe unfold

its great plan to us. OK? You don't have to decide which boy. I
don't have to sort out Scott.'

'OK,' I said. I knew I could rely on Erin to come up with the
best advice.

Chapter 17

Three Perfect Dates

I met Tyler in a café just off Portobello Road at around four-thirty. It was Tyler's choice – a funky old place with big squashy sofas and a big fire at the far end. He bought us hot chocolates with marshmallows on the top and then we bagged a sofa near the fire, settled back and got down to the business of getting to know each other.

'So you first,' he said and leaned back into the cushions.

'Er . . . I was born in India. We've lived in five places so far. Um. I'm a Gemini. I . . . what do you want to know?'

Tyler smiled. 'Start with telling me about all the places you've lived in.'

Once I got started, there was no shutting me up as he appeared to be genuinely interested in the wanderings of my family, who they were and what they did. After that he prompted me with questions to continue about what I was into, who my friends were, what I wanted to do when I left school. I felt very flattered by his attention. His eyes didn't wander around the café at all as I talked, the way that some boys do.

'You'll make a great journalist,' I said when I realised that I'd been talking non-stop about myself for almost an hour.

He smiled. 'I like people. Always have.'

'OK, now it's my turn,' I said. 'Tell me everything!'

He sat forward and said, 'OK. I'm nineteen, I grew up in New York though my family are from St Lucia, which of course you know having spent time there —'

'Just think, we might have been on the same beach there once,' I commented.

He shook his head. 'I think I'd have noticed you even when you were four,' he said, and looked at me in a way that made me blush.

'Do you ever go back?' I asked.

'Whenever I can. My grandparents still live there.'

'Brothers and sisters?'

'Two brothers, one sister, and we live in Queen's Park.'

I wanted to ask him other things like: Do you have a girlfriend? What do you look for in a girl? But I felt that it wasn't the time for more personal questions. Not yet.

'OK, so what are you into?'

'Well, as you know, I want to be a journalist. I want to make a difference. The right words can change things, make people think.' As he talked more about what he was into, the thing that struck me was how passionate he was about the environment and doing something to make a difference to the planet. He seemed so well informed about things like carbon footprints, and landfills and the greenhouse effect, I felt like a light-weight besides him. It was so interesting to hear him talk, and I realised that intelligent and well-read would be high on my list of what I wanted in a boyfriend from then on. As the afternoon progressed, I liked him more and more and was feeling a definite tingle of chemistry. I liked the thoughtful expression in his eyes, especially when he looked at me. Not to mention his fabulous mouth. *I wonder what he's like to kiss,* I thought to myself when he went to replenish our hot chocolates. *And I wonder if he'll try and kiss me today.*

'How about a movie?' he asked when he came back and sat next to me. 'They're showing *It's a Wonderful Life* at the Gate cinema down the road.'

'That's my favourite Christmas movie,' I said.

'One of mine too. I could watch it over and over. Be good to see it on the big screen though.'

'Let's do it,' I said.

After ringing home to check in with Mum, our afternoon drink turned into a longer date. We sat in the movie house and ate ice creams and, although he didn't put his arm around me or even hold my hand, it felt good to sit next to him in the dark, our thighs touching.

After the movie, we went and bought fish and chips and, when we went to pay, I got out my purse.

'No, let me get these,' he said. 'My treat.'

'Absolutely not,' I said. 'I want to get this. You've paid for the movie, the ice cream and the hot chocolates. You have to let me get something; besides, I wanted to say thank you for rescuing me that day.' I also wanted him to know that I wasn't someone who expected him to pay for everything all the time – I know students don't have a lot of money.

We went out of the shop, found a bench and ate our fish and chips in a companiable silence.

'You know one thing I like about you,' he said as I ate my last chip. 'You enjoy your food. There are so many girls who are so picky about what they can and can't eat, always on a diet. Not a lot of fun.'

'Well you've picked all my favourites today,' I said, glancing at my watch, 'so I couldn't resist. And I was starving and, oh, it's late. I'd better be getting home. I promised I'd be back around now.'

'I'll walk you home,' he said. We got up, put our chip papers into a bin and set off in the direction of where I lived. As we did, he casually took my hand. 'One thing I didn't ask you,' he said. 'Um. Do you have a boyfriend?'

'Not at the moment. Do you have a girlfriend?'

'No,' he replied, and he tucked my hand into his arm. It felt like the most natural thing in the world. 'Do you think it was fate bringing us together that day you got mugged?'

'Maybe, but I wish it had chosen a less violent way – like we could always have met in the queue at Costa.'

'Ah, but we might have never spoken to each other so

something good came from it, and we missed each other on that beach in St Lucia,' he said and he smiled a big smile.

I squeezed his arm to let him know that I agreed.

When we got to the corner of my road, he came to a stop, turned to me and put his hand gently under my chin tilting my face up to look at him. As he gazed down into my eyes, I felt a warm rush in my stomach and, when his lips touched mine a moment later, it felt completely right and comfortable. I kissed him back and when we seperated, we were both smiling at each other.

He made a half nod. 'Nice,' he said.

'Very,' I replied, and then we both stood there grinning like idiots because neither of us could think of anything else to say. And then he laughed and said, 'Let's do that again.' He leaned forward and kissed me again, a longer kiss and it felt even better. Like we were made to kiss each other.

In the middle of our third snog, I felt someone tugging on the back of my jacket and turned to see Dylan standing behind me. 'And who's this?' he asked in a funny, prim manner.

'Dy*lan*!' I groaned.

'Yes. So who is this?'

'None of your business. Clear off,' I said.

Tyler laughed. 'The name's Tyler. You must be India's brother.'

'Yes he is,' I said. 'My very annoying little brother.'

Dylan shook his hand. 'Oh yeah. I should have known. Good to meet you, Tyler. You're the one who helped India the day she got mugged, aren't you?'

Tyler nodded.

Dylan looked back at me. 'We all try to look after her you know.'

I gave him a gentle shove. 'That's very sweet of you. Now push off.'

Dylan hovered close by. 'It's late and you've been gone ages.'

'So? What's it to you?' I asked and turned back to Tyler. 'Dylan might look like my brother but he's actually my prison warder.'

'I see. In that case, I'd better be going,' said Tyler and he turned to Dylan and gave him a salute. 'Over to you, sir,' he said, then he turned back to me, kissed me lightly on the forehead and set off down the road.

I felt like I was smiling inside and out. Apart from my irritating brother, it had been the perfect day and the perfect date.

On Tuesday after school, I met Joe in Costa. He looked pleased to see me but slightly awkward.

'Hi,' he said. 'I wasn't sure that you'd come.'

'Why wouldn't I?' I asked.

He shrugged. 'Last time we spoke, you seemed a bit . . . well . . .'

'Pissed off with you? I guess I was. I was fed up with boys and not ever knowing where I stand.'

Joe pulled a package out of his bag. 'This is for you. It's some music that I like. A compilation. Says a few of the things that go on in my mad head.'

I took the CD and felt touched that he'd made it for me specially. 'Thanks.'

As we looked into each other's eyes, all the usual feelings I had for him came back and, unlike last time, I didn't shut them out. A part of me felt bad. Only a couple of days before, I'd been looking into Tyler's eyes, but I quickly let his image go. *Relax*, I told myself. *I haven't made any promises to anyone. It's early days with Tyler and Bruno. I am doing what Erin told me to, going with the flow.*

'Are you OK?' asked Joe. 'You look worried about something.'

'Me? No. Not really. No. Usual stuff.'

'Yeah, school. The show. But it's all looking good, isn't it?'

'It's looking great,' I replied.

Joe smiled. 'Remember what a hard time the scenery team gave you when you were first appointed as leader?'

'God yeah. Andrea Ward hated me.'

'Only because she's a control freak and thought that the scenery was her baby. I think she rates you now.'

'Really?'

'Yeah. Well you're good at art. You have a talent and you've pulled the team together. I wanted to say that on the night, though, we boys can handle the scenery changes and you girls can sit out front.'

'I don't mind helping shift stuff.'

'Too many people backstage if the whole team is there. We'll be fine. You sit and enjoy the show. You've done your bit. Hey, I'm starving. Fancy a pizza?'

'Um . . . yeah, OK.'

We got our things, went over the road and bought a pizza to share. As we ate it, we chatted about school and had a laugh at various bits of gossip about the show and it felt so good to be with him, like we'd been the best of friends for ever and could talk about anything. It was like he got me. After we'd finished eating, it began to rain. But not just rain, this was torrential and neither of us had an umbrella. He grabbed my hand and we ran down the pavement, and into a shop doorway to take shelter. It was raining so hard that it was splashing up from the pavement and streams of water were flowing down the road into the drains as lightning flashed and thunder boomed overhead. It made me laugh as we were both soaked with rain dripping off our faces.

'God, I must look a sight,' I said, trying to brush my wet hair away from my face.

Joe glanced over. He looked gorgeous with his hair slicked back, his face shiny from the rain and water droplets on his eyelashes. He gently pushed me back against the shop door and looked into my eyes – and I knew we were both feeling the same. It was amazing, like bubble bursts of sweetness exploding inside me. We leaned forward at the same time and fell into a passionate kiss that seemed to go on for ever. Then Joe pulled me out of the doorway right into the rain and kissed me again, and it felt exhilarating to be there, getting soaked through and yet feeling the warmth of his body pressing into mine. When we drew apart, we seemed out of breath then we started laughing and laughing.

'I'd better get you home,' he said and took my hand. We ran almost all the way home. At the same corner of the street where I'd stood with Tyler, Joe kissed me again and the sensation he caused in me went from the tip of my toes to the top of my head.

'You'd better go home too,' I said. 'You're getting soaked as well.'

He grinned. 'It's been worth it,' he said, but he did go when I pushed him gently away. As I turned to go into the pathway that led to the house, I thought, *I hope no neighbours or Dylan have been watching! Two different boys in three days, they'll think I am awful.*

When I let myself in, Mum came out of the kitchen. 'India. Oh Lord, did you get caught in that storm? Come on, get those clothes off. You must be freezing.'

But I wasn't. I had a wonderful warm feeling inside and I knew in my heart that, whatever was between Joe and me, it was really special.

Bruno flew in on Friday morning. He'd sent a text earlier in the week asking that I keep Saturday free for him. He wanted to do all his business first and get it out of the way so that we had time together. He suggested that we meet at his hotel and asked that I show him a little of London before he flew back on Sunday.

I got the tube to Green Park and, in my head, I was rehearsing my speech to him – that I only wanted to be friends and that a long-distance love affair wasn't a good idea and that we were both too young to commit. Since my date with Joe, I couldn't stop thinking about him and, every time I remembered the way that he'd grabbed me and kissed me in the rain, I felt my stomach flip over.

A doorman in a top hat opened the door as I approached the hotel and, as I entered the reception area, I felt slightly intimidated by how posh it was, with marble floors and enormous expensive-looking flower arrangements and smart people passing through. I was glad that I had borrowed Mum's three-quarter-length peacock-blue velvet coat to wear over my jeans – it looked like it had cost a bomb, although I knew she'd got it in a second-hand shop near Portobello Road. Luckily I didn't have to wait long until Bruno appeared from a lift at the back of the reception area. He was wearing his stylish coat and red scarf, and his face lit up when he saw me and I felt myself beaming too. I had forgotten how extraordinarily good-looking he was – something that a couple of other girls waiting in reception noticed too as they were obviously checking him out and whispering to each other. He didn't even notice them and came rushing towards me and wrapped me in a big bear hug. 'India, at last.'

'Er, hi Bruno,' I said, breathing in his light lemony scent and I remembered how good it had felt to be close to him. *Joe*, said a voice in my head, *you're in love with Joe remember? Not today, I'm not,* said a different voice. *What's going on?* said a third voice. *Oh, I'll think about it later. Go with the flow. Go with the flow.*

'How have you been? Missed me?' said Bruno as he put his

arm around me and steered me towards a room full of overstuffed sofas and leather chairs.

'I did and then I didn't,' I said. 'I . . . I thought you'd forgotten me.'

'*Never*,' he said. 'I think about you all the time and was cursing that I couldn't call you every day when I lost my phone. But how are you? You look beautiful.'

'I'm fine,' I said. 'A bit mad but fine. So what would you like to do?'

Bruno opened his arms and said, 'London!'

And so started the most fantastic day. Outside the Ritz hotel, we hopped on to one of the red open-topped tourist buses and sat upstairs. Although it was chilly, it was a lovely clear day and we sat close, snuggled up, and laughed at the bus driver's hysterical commentary about London. *Tyler would love this*, I thought when the guide filled us in on the history of the buildings and streets that we passed through. It was interesting to hear how much of old London had burned down in the great fire in 1666. We passed St Paul's cathedral and got off the bus at Tower Bridge. Bruno was well impressed by the Tower of London, and it made me shiver to think about all the people who had been executed or kept in the dungeons there.

After the Tower we caught a boat to Tate Britain, and, even though it was still cold, it was another excuse to cuddle up to him. Somewhere on the trip, my speech about just being friends seemed to have flown away, and I couldn't help wanting him to kiss me so that I could remember how it was when we were in

Ravello and find out if I'd imagined how fantastic it had been. Having snogged Tyler and Joe since I'd last seen Bruno, his kisses had faded in my mind and I needed to experience them again to see how he compared to the other two boys. At least that was what I was telling myself. He didn't seem in any hurry to kiss me though, and was content to hold my hand or put his arm around me like a protective uncle. It was very frustrating – like being out with one of my brother Lewis's friends. At the Tate Britain gallery, we spent an hour or so wandering around the rooms looking at the art and sculpture there. *Joe would love this*, I thought as we walked through a stunning exhibition of portraits. *I should come here with him*. Thinking about Joe made me feel sad and irritated. If he'd only get over his stubborn refusal to commit, we could do all sorts of great things together at the weekends. See exhibitions, go for walks, go to the movies. But he *doesn't* want to be in a relationship, I reminded myself, so you might as well enjoy being with someone who *does* want to be with you.

'And next is going to be a surprise,' said Bruno after we'd had enough of looking at paintings and we were standing on the steps outside the gallery. I took a step towards him, looked into his eyes and tilted my face up to his in the hope that he'd take the hint and *kiss* me, but he didn't. For a moment, I felt my confidence flounder, maybe Joe wasn't that into me and maybe Bruno wasn't either. Maybe I come on too strong or played it all wrong or something.

Bruno dashed on to the pavement where he hailed a taxi and

asked for a restaurant which I didn't catch the name of. I followed him down the steps and got into the cab and felt marginally better as we sat and held hands and watched the world go by. *Beats travelling by tube,* I thought as I took in the busy streets, the Christmas lights and the shoppers dashing about. *Now he's going to kiss me surely,* I thought.

But he didn't.

We drove past Buckingham Palace and up past St James's Park, and all the time Bruno was looking out of the window enthusing about the sights. *Never mind the sights,* I thought. *What about me!*

As the cab went through Trafalgar Square, it looked so Christmassy with the huge trees reaching up to the sky and the lights all around. It was then that, at last, Bruno put his arm around me and leaned towards me. He nuzzled into my neck and nibbled the bottom of my ear. Then he leaned further in, lifted my hair and kissed the nape of my neck. It felt exquisite. No one had ever done that before and I decided there and then that it was going to be my favourite thing, ever. Neck kissing. Even better than Häagen-Dazs ice cream. And then he kissed me properly, gently at first but then he pressed harder and I felt myself melting into him. It was wonderful, like I was falling into a warm velvety tunnel and nothing else existed except the sensation of being kissed. I put my hands up to the back of his neck and ran my fingers through his hair and he moaned softly. *Ohmigod,* said a voice at the back of my head. *I love three boys.* But I didn't let that put me off. Neither Joe nor Tyler was my proper boyfriend and it felt good to be back in Bruno's arms. Voices in the back of my head were saying, *Joe, Tyler, Joe, Tyler,* but I told them very firmly to shut up.

After a while, the cab drew up outside a grand-looking building on the Strand. Yet another doorman opened the door for us and we entered an amazing room with high ceilings and a floor that was black and white marble, which gave the place a church-like feel. No one was praying though – at the tables, people were busy chatting and eating and drinking and having a good time.

'Afternoon tea,' said Bruno as a smart girl dressed in black came forward to take our coats.

'Yumscious,' I said and told myself not to feel nervous. It felt so grown-up and formal, a million miles away from the cosy cafés where I usually hung out with my mates or Joe or Tyler.

'It used to be a bank apparently,' said Bruno. A waiter led us to a booth to the right of the restaurant where we took our seats and, moments later, yet another waiter handed us menus.

Well it sure is different to Costa or Starbucks, I thought.

Bruno glanced at the menu. 'The full works?' he asked.

'Sure,' I said. I wasn't sure what the full works was going to be, but I didn't want to sound like it was my first time in a place like this.

It arrived a short time afterwards. A plate of finger sandwiches, another plate of scones with pots of jam and cream and *another* plate full of the most divine, looking pastries. *I am going to get as fat as a pig,* I thought, helping myself to my first pastry, *and I don't care*. Bruno and I ate every scrap, then sat back and rubbed our tummies and laughed. I noticed a bunch of girls on a nearby table eyeing Bruno with admiration, so I reached over and took his hand and he lifted it to his lips and kissed it. I felt proud to be with him and, as I had in Ravello, once again it seemed like I was in a romantic movie with the lead man. *He makes everywhere seem glamorous,* I thought.

After our tea, it was six o'clock and Bruno had to go and meet some of the people to do with his father's hotel business. I was going to get the tube home but he insisted on getting me a cab. When the waiter came over and said that the taxi was waiting for me, Bruno paid the bill (I did offer to contribute but he wouldn't hear of it and, when I saw the bill, I was relieved because I didn't have enough money on me or even in my savings box!) and then we went out on to the pavement. He put his arms around me and pulled me close. '*Bella*, I hope you'll come over to Italy soon. Make the excuse to see your grandmother.'

'I'll do what I can,' I said. I had totally changed my mind since the morning and thought that maybe I could make a long-distance relationship work after all. What had I to lose? Not Joe and it was still early days with Tyler.

'And I will come over whenever I can,' he said. 'But for now, we are saying goodbye again.' He hugged me closer and we clung on to each other for a while until the taxi driver beeped his horn.

'This cab for you, miss?' he asked.

I nodded. 'I'd better go,' I said.

We had a last kiss that was gentle and tender and, when I got into the cab, I felt sad that our day was over. I turned to look out of the back window. Bruno was standing watching and then the cab pulled into the traffic and he was a blur on the pavement, one figure amongst many others. And then he was gone.

As the streets of London flashed past me, I thought back over my amazing week. Three boys, three perfect dates. Whatever next?

Chapter 18

Arghhhh!

The next two weeks were frantic with end of term coursework and completing the designs for the school show. Every spare moment was taken up with revision, painting scenery, meetings and rehearsals. In the meantime, Tyler sent a lovely postcard with a scene from the film *It's a Wonderful Life* on the front. On the back, he wrote, *Thinking of you*.

Bruno sent a dozen cream roses and a card that said, *Miss you, my bella India*.

Joe sent nothing, but he gave me a cheeky grin when I saw him in the corridor on the way to a rehearsal meeting.

'Been caught in any rainstorms lately?' he asked when he caught up with me.

'Not me. You?'

'Nothing like the one on Tuesday,' he said. 'That was really something, wasn't it?'

He looked deep into my eyes when he said that in a way that made my stomach lurch, and I knew what he meant and that he wasn't talking about the storm.

'Yes. I've never experienced anything like it.'

He raised a knowing eyebrow and grinned his lopsided grin. 'Me neither,' he said.

I love him, I thought as I went into double English where I spent the whole two periods replaying the storm and the kisses in my mind.

In maths, I relived the day I'd spent with Bruno. *I love him too*, I thought.

Finally it was the week of the end of term show and all our plans and hard work seemed to be coming together. I had just got home from school when Tyler phoned. Just hearing his voice made me remember how good I'd felt with him. *I could love him*, I thought. *Definitely maybe.*

And then he asked what I was doing on Friday night.

'School show,' I said.

'Oh the one you told me you'd done the scenery for?'

'Yes. Well, me and some others.'

'Can anybody go?'

'Yes. It's open to the public. Money goes towards a new science lab.'

'Are there tickets left?'

'Loads.'

'I'd love to come . . .'

Erk, I thought.

'India. You've gone quiet. Oh. Is there a problem?'

Duh, yeah, I thought. *Joe will be there. How will I explain Tyler to him? Or him to Tyler, especially when I've told Tyler that I don't have a boyfriend? And I still don't. Not really. Joe's not my boyfriend. Oh arrghhhhhhhhhhhhhhhhhhhhhh. I am sooooooo confused. Why did I have to meet them all at the same time. ANNOYing!*

'India?' Tyler prompted.

'Oh yes. Um. Oh God. Just I hate people seeing my work in case they don't like it,' I blustered. 'It would be like having a baby and someone saying, "Boy that's an ugly one!"'

Tyler laughed. 'I'm not going to do that. Art is a reflection of the person who made it so I expect to be impressed. Come on India, don't hide away. Let me be the judge, hey?'

'Er . . .'

'Is there some other reason that you're not telling me about why you don't want me to come?'

Out of the three boys, a relationship with Tyler would be the least complicated, I thought. *Bruno lives in Italy. Joe doesn't want a girlfriend. I'd be mad to turn such a lovely guy as Tyler down in the hope that something was going to happen with the other two when it might not come to anything with either of them.*

'No,' I blurted. 'I . . . No. Come. I'd love it.'

I'll get him a ticket and deal with the chance of him meeting Joe then, I thought as a feeling of panic hit my insides.

Chapter 19

Showtime

'Don't you feel at all guilty?' asked Zahrah from the bottom bunk bed where she was doing her eye make-up. We had decided to get ready for the show at her house because, out of our four homes, hers was nearest to school. Brook and I were squeezed on to the stool in front of the dressing table and Leela was behind us brushing her hair.

'Why should she?' said Leela as she put away her hairbrush and got out her lip-gloss. 'It's not like she's cheating on any of them.'

I gave up on trying to get any mirror space and I retreated to the end of the bottom bunk bed next to Zahrah. 'Well,' I said, 'that's what I keep telling myself. That it's early days with all of them and I haven't made any promises. However, I do think I need to decide soon and maybe let everyone know where I stand. If I was to carry on seeing them for much longer without telling, I think I'd start to feel like I *was* cheating especially as Tyler's coming to the show and may meet Joe.'

'But Joe is still Mr Non-Committal, isn't he?' asked Zahrah.

'Exactly,' I said. 'And Tyler hasn't asked me to be his steady girlfriend either. This will be only be the fourth time I've seen him.'

'OK, so what if all of them did suddenly want something more serious. Who would it be? Bruno, Joe or Tyler?' asked Zahrah.

I groaned. 'I don't know. I thought I really liked Joe best but he comes at a price and that price is spending a lot of time being frustrated with him. And it's early days with the others. How can I decide when they all have so much to offer?'

'Well what do *you* want?' asked Zahrah.

'I want the way all of them make me feel only with just one boy.'

Leela pulled a notebook out of her bag and ripped off a piece of paper. 'OK. Scores for kissing. Bruno?'

'Ten. He's a good kisser.'

'Tyler?'

'Um . . . yeah ten. He's also a good kisser. Different but good too. More gentle.'

'Joe?'

'Eleven.'

'OK, so it's Joe then,' said Leela.

'No,' Zahrah said. 'I mean a boy can be great kisser but mess your head up, right, India?'

'Right.'

'Yeah, 'course you said that, India,' said Leela. 'Has he never said anything about dating or commitment or going steady?'

I shook my head.

'And you've heard from all of them since the date?' asked Brook.

'Yes. Bruno sent roses and Tyler sent a card saying he'd had a lovely day.'

'Sweet,' said Brook. 'And Joe?'

'Nothing,' I replied. 'Actually, no. He did give me a CD he'd made for me but I haven't had time to listen to it yet. It's of some music that he said he liked, but . . . that's the sort of thing you do for a mate, isn't it?'

'No way,' said Leela. 'I think it's the sort of thing you do when you fancy someone.'

'Do you think?' I asked.

'Depends on the music,' said Zahrah. 'If it's a CD full of funeral music, he might be dropping a hint that your relationship is over.'

I laughed. 'Thanks for the vote of encouragement.'

'I'm just saying you need to hear the tracks he picked before you decide if he did it just as a mate thing,' said Zahrah.

'Maybe,' I said. 'Then again, it might not mean anything – although it is thoughtful of him. But . . . oh, I don't know, I like them all in different ways.'

Leela squeezed on to the bed between Zahrah and me. 'Different how?' she asked.

'Bruno makes me feel like a princess, which is lovely and so flattering. He wants the best for me, like he puts me on a pedestal. With Tyler, it's different. I feel safe with him and I look up to him. I admire him. I feel that I could learn from him; and Joe, well with Joe, it's like there's this amazing chemistry and we make each other laugh. Plus . . . it's like he gets me and we're equals.'

'I'd go for Tyler,' said Leela.

'I'd go for Bruno,' said Brook. 'He'll spoil you rotten.'

I turned to Zahrah. 'And you're going to say go for Joe, aren't you? Just to confuse things?'

Zahrah made one of her disapproving faces, shook her head and sucked in air. 'No. He could totally do your head in if you let yourself get too involved,' she said. 'We all know what he's like, Mr I-like-you-very-much-but-don't-want-to-commit, don't forget.'

'Yeah,' I said. 'I do love hanging out with him, though. But then I love hanging out with Bruno and Tyler, too. It's like how can you compare an orange with a pear, or a mango with a pineapple? Or say that one is better than the other? They each have different flavours and they're all good in their own ways.'

'My advice would be not to worry,' said Brook. 'Get tonight over with and I'm sure it will become clearer.'

Leela laughed. 'Yeah, clear like mud,' she said.

The atmosphere was buzzing in the school hall when we arrived and there was a lovely Christmassy smell of oranges and cinnamon from the mulled wine that was on sale to parents at the back of the hall. We found the places that had been kept for us at the front and then went our separate ways to greet guests and show them to their seats. All my family were coming en masse and would take up almost an entire row – I'd reserved seats for them and for Tyler. I couldn't see any sign of them yet, so I went backstage to see that everyone was OK. I had already spent the best part of the day working with the scenery team, back there making last minute adjustments and, on the whole, everything looked fantastic and my part of the job was over. I couldn't see Joe, but Harry and Tim from the team were there and gave me a wave.

'All under control, captain,' said Tim. 'Joe will be here in a mo, so it's over to us.'

Harry nodded. 'Yeah, you might as well just sit back and enjoy now.'

Out at the front, I could see that Tyler had arrived and was looking around the hall. 'Sit back and enjoy, yes,' I said – *and try and keep Tyler out of Joe's eyeline*, I thought.

As soon as I emerged from backstage, Brook came up to me and glanced in Tyler's direction. 'Ohmigod, is that him?' she asked. 'If you don't want him, I'll have him, no prob.'

Tyler spotted me and waved. I glanced around to see that Joe wasn't in the vicinity then went to meet him with Brook not far behind, and suddenly Leela and Zahrah appeared too. 'Hey,' I said. 'Um, these are my mates, Zahrah, Brook and Leela.'

The girls stood there grinning like idiots and then Ryan

appeared so Zahrah went off to show him his seat.

Leela batted her eyelashes at Tyler. 'Hey, you haven't got a brother, have you?' she asked.

'Two actually. Why? Want to meet them?'

Leela and Brook nodded. 'We had a challenge after half-term that we would find a boyfriend before Christmas,' said Leela. 'Brook and I have failed miserably.'

'Miserably,' said Brook. She made her bottom lip wobble and looked up at Tyler from downcast eyes. I laughed. It was funny to see them both go into major flirtation mode.

He laughed too. 'And what about you, India? How have you fared?'

Leela gave me a cheeky look so I kicked her ankle. 'Ouch,' she said. 'What?'

'Er . . . you shouldn't have told Tyler about that,' I said. 'He'll think that I manufactured my mugging just to meet him.'

Tyler pretended to look shocked. 'Did you?'

'No way,' I said and he smiled as I checked my watch. 'Hey. Come on, it's almost time. We'd better go in and take our seats.'

Tyler took my hand and together we walked towards the front of the hall. I turned back and made a 'what can I do?' face at Leela and Brook who were following behind us. They both held their sides and did fake laughing, like they found the situation very funny. As we took our seats, there was the hum of people chatting and I saw an usher showing Mum and Dad and the rest of the family to the row behind Tyler, Brook, Leela and me. Soon after, the lights went down and the audience grew quiet. I turned to do a family count: Mum, Dad, Lewis, Ethan, Jessica (for once having a night off from the twins), Aunt Sarah, Kate, her boyfriend Tom, and Dylan. I was about to turn back when I noticed Brook's mum was sitting at the end of the row with a handsome middle-aged man with silver hair who looked vaguely familiar. She waved when she saw me.

'Mom's new boyfriend,' said Brook. 'The biologist from the dating site, remember?'

'Oh yeah.'

'She's in love. It's nauseating.'

'I think it's nice.'

'You don't have to put up with her acting like a fifteen-year-old with a crush,' said Brook. 'It's not right. It should be me with the boyfriend.'

'Your turn will come,' I said.

She made a pouty face. 'Not the way you and my mom are bagging all the talent.'

The curtains drew back, some Indian music struck up and the cast for *The Boy Friend* danced on Bollywood style in a blast of colour. They looked wonderful and the scenery was perfect, creating just the right ambience for the show. It was an explosion of energy, dance and song. Tyler laughed and applauded and appeared to enjoy every moment of it.

'Great scenery,' he whispered at one point and I felt proud to have done something that he could admire.

At the end, the audience gave a standing ovation. The cast did two encores and then they called for everyone who'd helped in the show to come on stage. Joe, Harry and Tim were shoved on from the wings and Joe caught my eye and beckoned me up. Tim and Harry were calling to Ruth, Gayle and Andrea who were the other team members.

'Go on,' said Leela. 'Go and take a bow. The Bollywood thing was all your idea after.'

I got up and made my way on to the stage with the others, and Joe took my hand and Gayle's and we took the bows together. As the clapping died down, we trooped off into the wings where everyone was high on adrenalin and congratulating each other.

'Good show, well done everybody,' said Mr Bailey, the art teacher, and he applauded the cast, who seemed very happy with the way it had gone.

I turned to go back to the audience as I could see that people were beginning to leave the hall and Tyler was standing on his own.

Joe caught up with me at the top of the stairs from the stage. 'Who's the guy?' he asked.

'What guy?' I replied.

'The guy who's been holding your hand all through the show. Is he the one you met in Italy?'

'No. That's Bruno. That guy is, er . . . that's Tyler. He's the one who came to my rescue when I was mugged.'

Joe's expression became serious as he looked out at where Tyler was standing. 'Your hero,' he said.

'Something like that.'

Joe leaned forward, took a strand of my hair and tucked it behind my ear. 'You going out with him now?' he asked casually.

I shrugged. 'Um. Early days,' I replied, pulled away and skipped down the steps to see that Tyler had turned around and had been watching us.

Tyler and I began to walk out of the hall when he stopped. 'So who was that?' he asked.

'Who?'

'That guy you were talking to?'

'Who him? Joe Donahue. He's just a guy on the scenery team. Nobody.'

'Didn't look that way,' said Tyler. 'Looked serious.'

'Not at all. He's, er . . . in the Sixth Form here.'

I turned around to see if Joe was still on the stage. He wasn't. He had come down behind me and had started stacking chairs to our left. His expression wasn't giving anything away, but he was close enough to have heard what I just said.

Oops, I thought.

Chapter 20

Christmas Eve

Cinnamongirl: Erin. At last. I've been calling and texting you. And so verily, tis Christmas Eve and the season to be jolly, but tis raining here and I need my brolly. Haha, I'm a poet and I don't know it.

Irishbrat4eva: Yeah, I got your messages. Been a lot going on.

Cinnamongirl: Why? What's happened? Is it Scott again? Are you OK?

Irishbrat4eva: Yeah I'm OK. All came to a head. Party down the road. Scott was there necking it back as usual and acting the big man smoking dope and then he disappeared. We found him in the garden, this time in a really bad way, worse than ever before. Was scary. Really scary. The guy who was having the party, Fergie, he called Scott's mum and she came and took him to the hospital where they pumped his stomach. She was so mad, she contacted all his mates and found out what had been going on.

Cinnamongirl: Ohmigod! Did she talk to you?

Irishbrat4eva: Oh yes.

Cinnamongirl: Did you tell about him?

Irishbrat4eva: Yes, actually I wish I'd done it sooner. I wish I'd written an anonymous letter to her or something instead of writing to him, because he could have died if we hadn't gone looking for him and found him. The doctor said that a boy his age, his liver couldn't take the amount of alcohol he'd consumed and he could have died.

Cinnamongirl: Wow. But he's going to be OK?

Irishbrat4eva: Think so. They're going to keep an eye on him.

Cinnamongirl: He's going to be mad that you ratted on him.

Irishbrat4eva: I know, but at least he's alive and maybe this will scare him into being more sensible.

Cinnamongirl: I hope so. God, Erin. I'm so sorry you've been having such a hard time.

Irishbrat4eva: Not as bad as what Scott has been going through. Hold on . . . Mum's calling me, someone's on the landline. Might be news of Scott. Later?

Cinnamongirl: Later.

I signed off, got changed into my Christmas jumper, which is red with a leaf of holly embroidered on the front. It's totally naff but all our family revel in who can wear the worst Christmas outfit on Christmas Eve. I added some Christmas tree earrings that I'd bought from the local supermarket then went down to join everyone. Christmas Eve is my favourite day of the whole season. I love it because there is all the anticipation of Christmas coming the next day. The shops are shut, people have stopped work, school is over, it's the holidays and, after the frantic last-minute shopping and preparation, a feeling of quiet settles everywhere as people take to their homes. All our family like to get together on December the twenty-fourth for a sing-song and Mum and Dad work hard to make wherever we are look festive. When I went downstairs, the red and gold Christmas tree was twinkling in the hall and Aunt Sarah had lit loads of candles and turned off all the electric lights so that the house was bathed in a warm golden glow. Best of all, Mum had bowls of chocolates and fruits and nuts on the sideboard in the living room for people to help themselves to. I took a white Belgium chocolate and popped it into my mouth.

I was beginning to feel clearer about what I was going to do about my complicated love life. Bruno had sent me a lovely silver charm bracelet in a blue box with a 'T' on it. Mum said that it was from a shop called Tiffany's and, although it was beautiful, it made me even more resolute to tell him that I wasn't ready for a relationship with him yet. I hadn't even had one serious boyfriend so far and didn't want my first one to live so far away especially as, despite my recent string of dates with different boys, I did think that once I was in a relationship I wouldn't mess around. It wouldn't be much fun if I only saw Bruno once a year for a short time. Plus, if he was going to keep sending me expensive presents and giving me treats, I knew there would come a time when I felt bad that I couldn't return his attention and would maybe feel obligated, and I didn't want to go there.

Tyler was spending Christmas with his family in St Lucia and had flown off several days earlier after having set up a date in the calendar for next year. I liked him a lot and there was no reason that I shouldn't go out with him because Joe still hadn't said anything about us going steady. I'd decided to cut myself some slack and leave the decision-making about him until after Christmas. There wasn't anything I could do so I wasn't going to fret over it and ruin the holiday.

As the family settled around the piano ready for our first song, my mobile bleeped that there was a text message. It was from Erin and she wanted me to go back to MSN. I promised Mum that I wouldn't be long and raced back up the stairs to my computer.

Irishbrat4eva: Sorry about before.
Cinnamongirl: S'OK. Was it news of Scott?
Irishbrat4eva: More than that, it was Scott. They let him out of hospital.
Cinnamongirl: How did he sound?

Irishbrat4eva:	Subdued but . . . OK, I think. He actually apologised for being a dickhead.
Cinnamongirl:	Wow. That's something for him.
Irishbrat4eva:	I know. He didn't say much about last night but, when I asked how he was, he said: New Year soon, New chapter.
Cinnamongirl:	That sounds positive, doesn't it?
Irishbrat4eva:	Yeah, for him. He's not a boy of many words. New chapter. I think I got what he was saying.
Cinnamongirl:	Fingers crossed.
Irishbrat4eva:	Yeah. Hey, I haven't asked about your show. How did it go?
Cinnamongirl:	Really good. A great success.
Irishbrat4eva:	Fantastic. How are the three lieges, yon loves of thy life?

I breathed a sigh of relief. I knew Erin was feeling better the moment she lapsed back into our Shakespearian speak.

Cinnamongirl:	Verily, I am perplexed. My per has never been so plexed in fact. Tyler was lovely. He wants to be my number one liege, but Joe didst not look happily upon the situation.
Irishbrat4eva:	What about yon liege from the land of pasta?
Cinnamongirl:	Methinks that long-distance love can't work in the long run, though it saddens my heart.
Irishbrat4eva:	Thou speaketh wisely. And thou canst always meet

up with him later when you are an international artist jetting the globe. Hmm. So that's one down, two left. Who doth thou choose?

Cinnamongirl: I don't know. It's strange because, now that Joe sees that I may have someone else, he has been acting keen.

Irishbrat4eva: Verily it is because love is a dance. You move forward, he moves away, he moves forward, you move away. He probably feels safe now, safe that you're not desperate for only him and so he feels able to advance. That's when things start to happen.

Cinnamongirl: Verily. Remember a few months ago, I was wondering how you knew if you were really in love.

Irishbrat4eva: Yeah. And how dost thou?

Cinnamongirl: I don't know. But I do know that it's possible to love people in different ways. That I am sure of. As there is the pineapple, so is there the mango.

Irishbrat4eva: Verily, thou hast been at the Christmas sherry methinks. Ah. I get you. Boys. Different flavours. Hmm. I guess thou needn't makest thy mind up just yet, tis Christmas and the season to be jolly.

Cinnamongirl: Ding dong verily on high.

Irishbrat4eva: And a ding dong to you too, and fare thee well for my family dost beckon me down to attend yon church. Speaketh soon.

Cinnamongirl: Fare thee well and may your dreams be full of fruit.

Irishbrat4eva: Party on pineapple girl and may your melons be plentiful. Oh, don't go yet. Woah thy horses. How did Leela, Zahrah and Brook fare in Leela's love challenge?

Cinnamongirl: Verily Zahrah has been smote by the arrows of lurve and she and Ryan are in smooch heaven.

Irishbrat4eva: Hah! And she was the cooleth of them all.

Cinnamongirl: Verily. Never say never.

Irishbrat4eva: And yon others?

Cinnamongirl: Sadly the land is barren when it comes to yon handsome knights to take their hands. And it is not for lack of looking.

Irishbrat4eva: Verily. For I too doth search but to no avail. Tell them it will soon be a New Year and, as Scott says, it bringeth a new chapter for us all.

Cinnamongirl: I will.

Irishbrat4eva: And now I really do fare thee well. Laters.

Cinnamongirl: Laters.

Downstairs, I heard the doorbell ring so I shut my computer and ran downstairs to see who was there. Joe's mum, Charlotte, had just arrived with a bunch of presents. Behind her was Joe, who gave me a cheeky grin.

'Merry wotnot,' he said.

'Same to you with tinsel on,' I replied but with a smile to show that I was pleased to see him.

In the living room, Dad began to play the piano and we all

went in and soon my family were singing carols with gusto, apart from Kate who looked on with disdain from her place on the end of the sofa where she was sitting with Tom, who wasn't singing either. Dad moved on to songs from famous musicals and I wondered whether Joe was finding the whole thing mad, but I decided that if he didn't like my family he wouldn't really like me so I sang along at the top of my voice and challenged him with my eyes to join in. He sat and listened for a while with an amused expression on his face and then joined in when Dad played 'Climb Every Mountain' from *The Sound of Music*. He had an awful voice and I put my fingers in my ears and he stuck his tongue out at me. When Dad went back to carols and began to play, 'Ding Dong Merrily on High', Joe got up and whispered, 'India, can we talk for a sec?'

'Sure,' I said and got up to follow him out through the hall and into the kitchen.

He shut the door behind us and turned to look at me. 'So?'

'So what?'

'Have you decided what you're doing?'

'What like my GSCE subjects? Yeah ages ago.'

Joe came and playfully wrung my neck. 'No. Not your GSCEs. You know I don't mean them. What about us? What about the guy I saw you with at the show?'

'Tyler? He's in St Lucia.'

'Wow. Lucky guy. So is it serious with him?'

I shrugged and decided to give him back some of the lines

he had given me ever since I met him. 'Early days but, you know, I'm young. I haven't even played the field yet. I don't want to commit to anyone.'

'But what about us? You know there's something special here.'

I nodded. 'Yes, but,' I indicated the door, 'through there are my family and my aunt Sarah and your mother, Charlotte. If we get involved and it doesn't work out, it wouldn't be good. No. Too close to home.' I said it in a light-hearted way though and with a twinkle in my eye so that he'd get that I was teasing him.

Joe nodded. 'Hah. Ouch. Yeah. Hmm. Sounds familiar. OK. You got me. So . . . what if a guy changes his mind? Is ready to take a risk?'

'Oh I don't know, Joe. I'm not a player. I don't believe in messing people around or cheating, but . . .' A thought hit me like a thunderbolt. 'Oh. My. God!'

'What?'

'I've just realised something. Ohmigod. About you. Ohmigod.'

'What?'

I couldn't say it to his face. I needed time to take it in, but what I had realised was that I was just the same as he was. And that I understood totally where he'd been coming from when he'd told me that he didn't want to get involved. When he'd said that he really liked me but didn't want to get tied down, well, he wasn't being rotten. He was being *honest*. His situation had been no different to mine now and I know that *I'm* not a love rat or a user. I just happened to meet three fantastic boys all around the same time.

I couldn't help it. I found myself grinning.

'What?' Joe asked.

'Nothing,' I said. 'Just . . . another thing I've realised that we've got in common.'

At that moment, the door burst open. It was Mum. She picked up a tray of mince pies from the table. 'Come on, you two, we're going to sing some more carols.'

Joe grinned. 'If you can't beat them, join them,' he said.

'Exactly,' I said and we followed Mum through the hall and towards the living room. Just before we went into the room, Joe caught my hand and pulled me back. I didn't resist and he quietly closed the living room door and pointed to the mistletoe that Mum had hung up from the ceiling the night before.

'So?' he asked.

I stepped forward.

No harm in a Christmas kiss. And a ding dong merrily on high, I thought as we leaned forward and melted into each other's lips.

Just before going to sleep that night, I was looking for a book in my school rucksack and I came across the CD that Joe had given me weeks ago. I put it in my CD-player and lay back on the bed.

He'd said that it was some music that expressed what was

going on in his head and a couple of tracks that he'd been into lately. I pressed Play and the sound of Neil Young's voice filled the room. '*I want to live with my Cinnamon Girl, I could be happy for the rest of my life with my Cinnamon Girl.*'

When Santa did his rounds that night, he would have seen that I'd fallen asleep with a big stupid smile on my face.

Find out more at www.piccadillypress.co.uk
Join Cathy's Club at www.cathyhopkins.com

Cathy Hopkins

Like this book?
Become a mate today!